T H O R N

HAVE YOU EVER WONDERED HOW BOOKS ARE MADE?

Fox & Ink Books (formerly UCLan Publishing) is an award-winning independent publisher. Based at the University of Lancashire, this Preston-based publisher teaches MA Publishing students how to become industry professionals using the content and resources from its business; students are included at every stage of the publishing process and credited for the work that they contribute.

The business doesn't just help publishing students though. Fox & Ink Books has supported the employability and real-life work skills for the University's Illustration, Acting, Translation, Animation, Photography, Film & TV students and many more. This is the beauty of books and stories; they fuel many other creative industries! The MA Publishing students are able to get involved from day one with the business and they acquire a behind-the-scenes experience of what it is like to work for a such a reputable independent.

The MA course was awarded a Times Higher Award (2018) for Innovation in the Arts, and the business was awarded Best Newcomer at the Independent Publishing Guild (2019) for the ethos of teaching publishing using a commercial publishing house. As the business continues to grow, so too does the student experience upon entering this dynamic master's course.

www.foxandinkbooks.com
www.foxandinkbooks.com/courses/
foxandink@lancashire.ac.uk

ALSO AVAILABLE BY A.F. HARROLD

Poetry

Things You Find in a Poet's Beard
The Book of Not Entirely Useful Advice
Pocket Book of Pocket Poems
Welcome to Wild Town (with Dom Conlon)
Midnight Feasts (as editor)
Poems for 7 Year Olds (as editor)
If I Met a Tiger (I'd Let It Eat Me)

Comedies

Fizzlebert Stump: the Boy Who Ran Away from the Circus and Joined the Library
Fizzlebert Stump and the Bearded Boy
Fizzlebert Stump: the Boy Who Cried Fish
Fizzlebert Stump and the Girl Who Lifted Quite Heavy Things
Fizzlebert Stump: the Boy Who Did PE in his Pants
Fizzlebert Stump and the Great Supermarket Showdown

Greta Zargo and the Death Robots from Outer Space
Greta Zargo and the Amoeba Monsters from the Middle of the Earth

Novels

The Imaginary
The Afterwards
The Song from Somewhere Else
The Worlds We Leave Behind

A.F. HARROLD

THORN

Cover illustration by SIMON PEMBERTON

Interior illustrations by MILLY CHAPPLE

Fox & Ink Books

Thorn is a Fox & Ink Books book

First published in Great Britain in 2026 by
Fox & Ink Books, part of the
University of Lancashire
Preston, PR1 2HE, UK

978-1-917894-15-9

9 8 7 6 5 4 3 2 1

Text design by Becky Chilcott.

A CIP catalogue record for this book is available from the British Library.

Printed and bound in Great Britain by Clays Ltd, Elcograf S.p.A.

For David Yates –
Let's make more things no one asked for – AFH

For Mum, Dad and Joe – MC

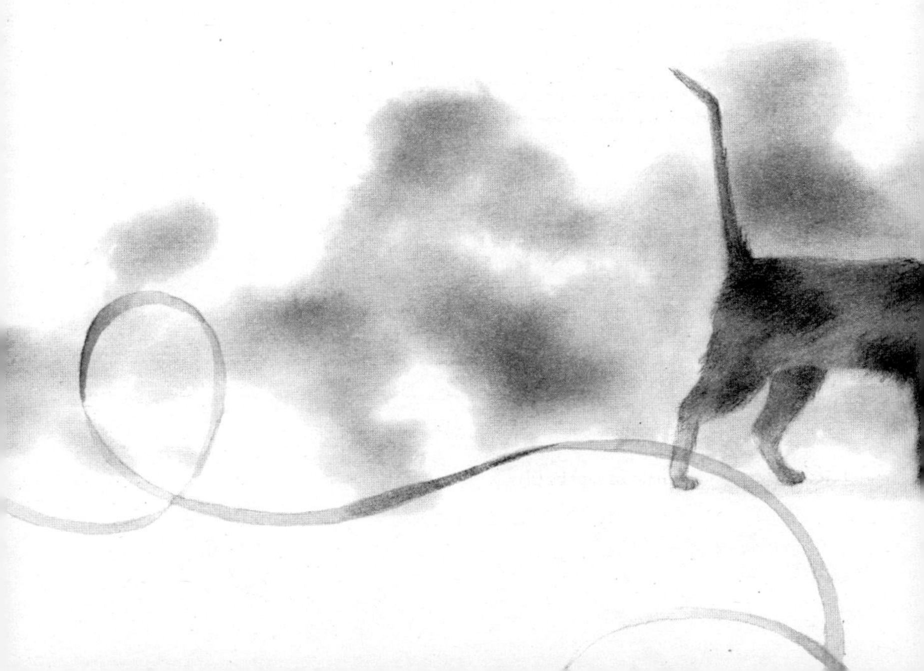

Kingfisher

That kingfisher jewelling upstream
seems to leave a streak of itself behind it
in the bright air. The trees
are all the better for its passing.

It's not a mineral eater, though it looks it:
It doesn't nip nicks out of the edges
of rainbows. – It dives
into the burly water, then, perched
on a Japanese bough, gulps
into its own incandescence
a wisp of minnow, a warrior stickleback.
– Or it vanishes into its burrow, resplendent
Samurai, returning home
to his stinking slum.

Norman MacCaig, from
The Poems of Norman MacCaig

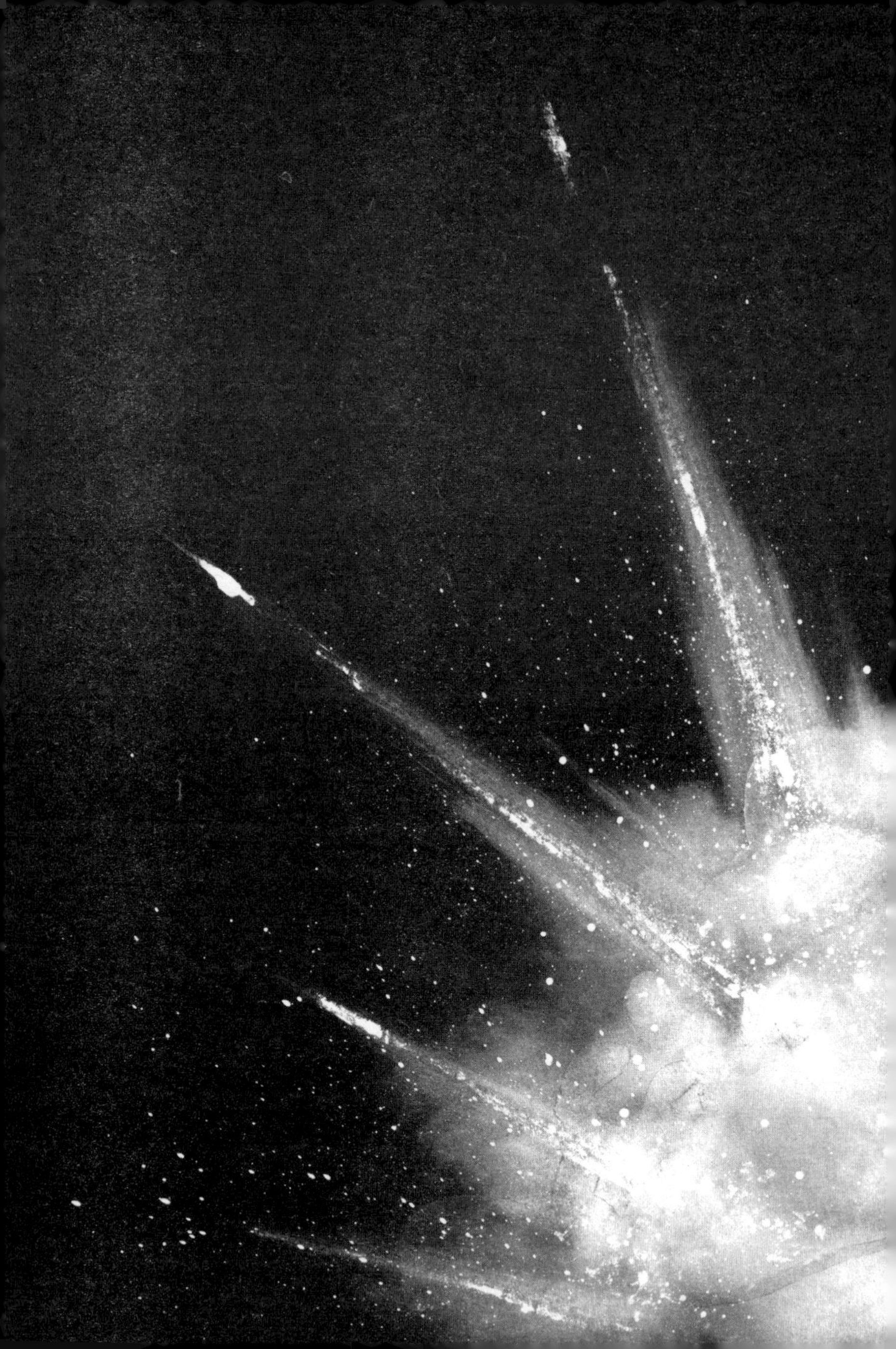

ZERO

THERE WAS AN explosion.

A bright light to begin things, and dust and darkness to follow.

And so the universe began.

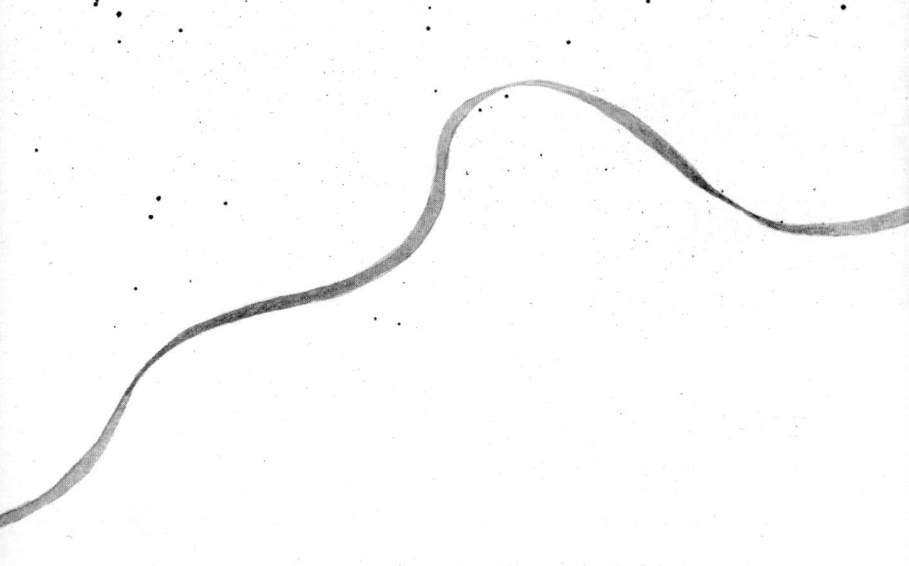

ONE

THORN WOKE UP.

The room was dark.

She heard a murmur and clinking from downstairs – distant noises that told her it must be morning.

Thorn shook her head and tried to remember what day it was, what classes would be rolling over the horizon to darken her mood.

Thursday, she thought. *I think it's Thursday.* The greyest of all days. The most slippery.

With Friday you knew where you were. The day before freedom, when no one expected anything much to matter, workwise.

Monday, Tuesday, Wednesday . . . well, you were just

dragging yourself up the hill of the week, slowly getting used to school routine after a couple of days of light and space.

But Thursday. Urgh. The plateau.

It was a day her timetable had decided to fill with double Maths, followed by Geography. Numbers and mud. Mud and numbers. Thorn did not thrill to this prospect.

She looked down at her body lying under the duvet in the dark room and wondered why she was looking down at her body lying under the duvet in the dark room.

Shouldn't she be *in* her body?

Shouldn't she *be* her body?

That was the first clue she had that something had gone sideways.

TWO

THE BEDSIDE CLOCK started flashing and ringing.

Thorn's body's arm flung itself out from under the duvet and slammed down on the poor device's head.

"I was only following orders," it said. "*Your* orders."

Thorn's body grunted, yawned, stretched, scratched, blinked and grunted again.

"Oh," said Thorn. "That's odd."

Her body slowly unfolded, pushing the duvet onto the floor, like a bed shedding its skin.

Then it swung its legs round, while still lying down, and let each foot fall, in turn, to the carpet.

Thonk!

Thunk!

“Ow,” said the carpet. “You could have warned me.”

“I tried,” said the alarm clock.

A hand gripped the edge of the mattress, and then another hand.

“Ugh,” said Thorn’s body, as it pulled itself into a sitting position.

This was not normal. Or rather, Thorn thought, it was exactly normal.

She recognised her getting-out-of-bed routine, step by step, only she usually had her eyes shut and could feel the creases of her pyjamas bunch and pinch under her back as she moved.

She had never watched it from outside before.

She thought she ought to be scared. *I ought to be scared.*

And then she thought, *Who is driving my body?*

And then, *It ought to be me, right?*

For a moment she felt unsure.

Thursdays were like that, but never before had they been like this.

There was a rapid, rising *thud-thud-thud* from outside, as someone came running up the stairs.

The door burst open like a sluice-gate of light, and Thorn's mum said, "Come on, sleepyhead. Get up. Get downstairs. I've put toast on." And then she was gone, into the bathroom, and the sound of the shower started singing.

Thorn said, "Wait, Mum, I think something's wrong," but she was too slow and too far away and her mum was long gone.

Her body, on the other hand, wobbled to its feet, dragged its fingers through its hair and began to swap pyjamas for school uniform.

Thorn turned away, to give her body some privacy, and went out onto the landing.

She moved without moving her legs, for she had no legs, just a sort of focus where her senses gathered, a *here* where she was looking from and hearing at. It was an odd thing, willing herself forwards – thinking and moving in one joint action – but it seemed to work.

She tried knocking on the bathroom door, but she didn't have hands, and the door didn't offer any resistance to her not-hands. She peered through and saw more than she wanted, so, instead, she just followed her body downstairs.

THREE

"DO I REALLY look like that from behind?" she asked, drifting down the stairs behind her body.

No one answered, but it was true. That *was* what she looked like from behind.

"Oh," she said. "I didn't think I was so . . . clumsy."

It was an odd word to pick, perhaps, but it was the word she found.

Her body bounced off the walls as it went down, like a pinball, or a bobsleigh, or a surprise party.

It wasn't awful. Her body looked like a normal person's body. She had the general idea of the shape and size of it right, but whenever she'd seen it, in the mirror, say, or in photos, it was always her front, which was just more . . . interesting.

The front had buttons and zips, school badges and her face. The back was mainly just a collection of flat blank undecorated expanses of cloth, with no distinguishing features at all.

But it wasn't *that* that was surprising. Not exactly. She'd seen other people's backs a million times. She knew what backs looked like. But she'd never really thought of herself, or of *her body*, as having a back like they did. After all, other people were other people, but she was Thorn.

Her body had made it to the kitchen and grabbed the two slices of toast right as they popped out of the toaster. They bounced from hand to hand, too hot, until her body dropped them on the table – no plate – which is exactly what Thorn would've done had it been her having the toast.

Her older brother, Gregor, tutted.

He was sitting on the other side of the table, poking a long spoon into a grapefruit.

A newspaper sat on the table beside his bowl. Its headline shouted: FRAGILE-MANN WINS 'ELECTION' IN NEXTDOOR COUNTRY. The picture crossed the fold, so she could only see the top of a man's head. Fluffy hair, like a dandelion about to tell the time, gently blowing.

A drop of stinging grapefruit juice landed on the paper.

"Ouch," it said. "That went in my eye."

Her brother ignored it, and spooned a sour, dripping spoonful into his mouth.

Thorn didn't much like him.

"Use a plate," he said, pointing at the toast, still chewing a mouthful of fruit mush.

"I'm saving on washing up," her body said.

Thorn nodded in agreement. Good point.

"You're getting crumbs everywhere."

"No, I'm not," said her body, licking one of its fingers and dabbing at the table-top.

"Disgusting," said her brother.

"I know you are," said her body, pulling a face and crunching into the toast at the same time. "But what am I?"

"So childish," said her brother.

"I *nom nom nom*," said her body, through a mouthful of toast.

Thorn wished *she* had some toast.

She didn't actually feel hungry, but toast would've been normal.

Being hungry would've been normal.

Being apart from your body was *not* normal.

Seeing them being so ordinarily breakfast-time-ish in the kitchen had grounded her for a minute, made her almost (but not really) forget how odd her day was being.

Crunch!

Toast.

Not-being-in-your-body.

Crunch!

Toast.

Not-being-in-your-body.

What's happened? she thought.

She counted the options on imaginary fingers.

One: maybe I'm a ghost.

Two: maybe I'm dreaming.

Three: maybe I've got a brain disease.

Four: maybe . . . um . . . maybe . . . I'm . . . um . . .

This was tricky.

It was definitely a Thursday.

FOUR

IT'S REALLY HARD to pinch yourself when you don't have hands.

FIVE

THEY WERE IN the car on the way to school.

Thorn was just sort of along for the ride, while her body sat in the passenger seat, clutching her schoolbag and tapping along to the car radio on the dashboard.

"Did you do your homework?" her mum said.

Thorn didn't remember what homework she'd had.

She was normally pretty good at remembering it. Not necessarily at *doing* it, or doing it *well*, but she always knew exactly what she was supposed to have done.

But this morning . . .

This morning she couldn't remember.

What did I do last night?

If it *was* Thursday today, then she probably had some

Maths due, and maybe some colouring-in for Mr Leech the geography teacher.

Maps?

She watched her body for a clue.

It was ignoring her mum and nodding with the music.

"*Hey girl!*" the radio sang. "*Did you do all your practice sums? / Hey girl! Binomial theorums?*"

"That doesn't really rhyme," Thorn told it. "That's not how you spell 'theorems'."

"You're one to talk," said the radio. "None of you rhymes. You're not even in time with your own body."

Thorn looked at the radio, sat in the middle of the dashboard, and she looked at her body and at her mum. Neither of them seemed to have heard it speak.

"*Teacher's in a mood, cos the kids are acting up. / There's not enough coffee in the coffee cup.*"

"What did you say?" said Thorn.

"I said," said the radio, in between guitar solos and traffic alerts, "you're having a difficult day."

"Do you know what's happened to me?"

"I'm just a tiny loop," the radio said. "I only notice things in the car. I don't know about the rest of it. Not how it all works."

"How come you've never spoken to me before?" Thorn said. "I've been in the car loads. Hundreds of times, probably, and you've never said a thing."

"I speak all the time," the radio said. "Maybe you were never in the mood to listen. Oh, hang on, here comes a good bit."

The music fell away, leaving just the drums and bass to drive the song on as the singer sang over the top: "*I think I ought to mention, / that you're gonna get detention / if you keep on ignoring / all the things you think are boring, / cos school's cool! / School's cool! / School rocks!*"

"I know this song," Thorn said, "and those aren't the words."

"No, probably not," said the radio, "but you look like you could do with some encouragement."

"You can see me? *Me* me?"

"No," said the radio. "I'm a radio. I don't have eyes."

Thorn felt even more confused as the school arrived and her body piled out onto the pavement.

She had been seen . . . well, had been noticed, at least. But not by anyone that mattered.

She was no closer to working out what had happened to her, and no closer to understanding why she felt so calm about her disembodiedness.

She knew she ought to be frantic, but she simply wasn't.

Is there something wrong with me? she thought, before laughing and saying, "Yep!"

Thorn followed her body into school.

SIX

THE CORRIDORS BUSTLED with teenagers in their dark uniforms, but Thorn just drifted through them, not being knocked this way or that, as her body bustled ahead of her.

She felt a faint memory of jealousy as she watched her body say, "Morning!" and smile at and nod at the other kids, all of whom she more or less knew.

Yesterday that had been her.

Today it was someone else. Someone else behaving just like her, just like she always did.

A fifth possibility suddenly stepped round the corner of her mind: *Maybe something has taken over my body and I, the me of the me of me, has been kicked out?*

That was the sort of spooky stuff that went on in the Nextdoor Country, or so the whispers always said. But she didn't think anyone *really* believed it, not in this day and age. But all the same, even the hint of a ghost of an idea of one of those freaks being in control of her body made her feel as if she ought to feel revolted.

She watched it stow some books in her locker (it knew the combination), and noted how it paused with its hand on the grey-painted metal, for a moment too long, staring into the jumbled dark mess with Thorn's eyes.

Stuck on the inside of the door was a sticker of a blue-orange glinting bird, wings spread, flying out.

A kingfisher, Thorn thought. *I don't remember sticking that there.*

Her body sighed.

A moment passed.

And then a voice Thorn recognised called her name, and her body slammed the door shut, spun on its heel and smiled a broad smile at Sam, her friend, who was shoving her way down the corridor.

Thorn didn't feel half as jealous as she thought she should, and she didn't feel a quarter as *scared* as she thought she should, either.

That's my body, she thought, as Sam and her body headed off.

And it's going about its business as if it doesn't need me. I should be screaming and shivering and pulling my hair out – terrified. What if I never get back in it? What if I'm left like this for ever?

She *knew* what it was to be scared, or angry, or revolted. She could *think* it, think these things. Could understand the why of them. But . . . she just wasn't *being* them.

Everything was . . . not fine, exactly, but sort of neutral. Even as it was odd.

Stranger and stranger, she thought.

By now the corridors had cleared, and so she drifted through the familiar door at the top of the Art block stairs and into her form room.

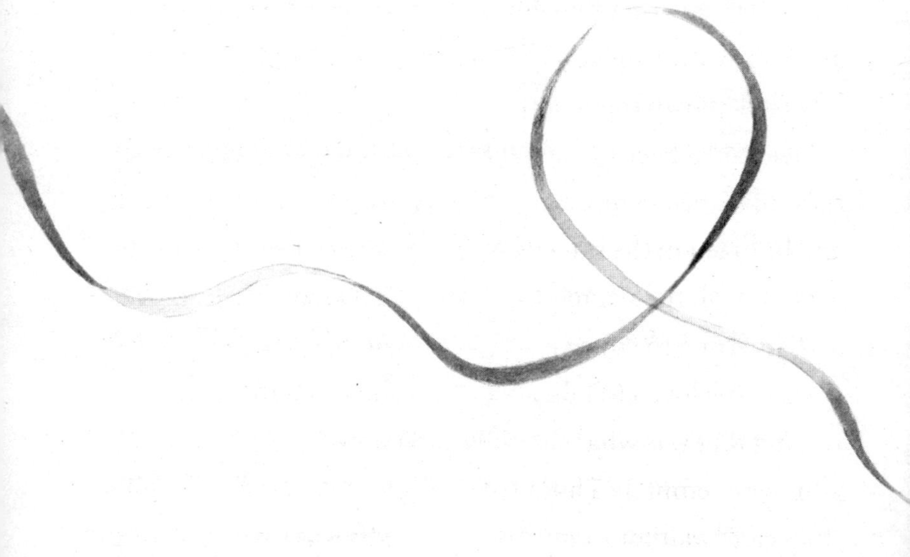

SEVEN

THORN'S BODY WAS over to the side, under the window that looked out over the woodwork huts, sat at a table with Sam and Katt.

She'd known them both for years.

They'd all been at the same primary school together, but they'd not been close back then. Since they'd arrived here, and been put in the same tutor group, they'd become friends, even though they didn't have a million things in common.

Sam loved to dance.

And she loved to talk about how she loved to dance.

And that was what she was doing now.

It was definitely Thursday.

"I can't wait for tomorrow night," she was saying, waving

a red liquorice lace in the air. "Daddy's taking me to the Blue Palace to see Swan Lake."

The Blue Palace was a theatre in the next town along. Swan Lake was a ballet.

Thorn's body knew these things, and nodded enthusiastically, but Katt said, "I thought the Palace was for shows. What've they got ducks there for?"

"Not ducks," said Sam, biting off an inch of liquorice. "*Swans*."

"OK," said Katt. "But they're basically the same thing. Just cos one's bigger and all white and can break your arm . . ."

"No one's breaking anyone's arm," Thorn's body interrupted. "They're dancing, dummy!"

A moment's silence.

"They've got dancing ducks? Gods! That sounds amazing. Do you think your dad will take me?"

Sam laughed and slapped the desk.

Thorn's body curled over laughing too.

Katt looked from one to the other, her face half-crumpling, half-frowning, as if to say, "What? What have I said now?"

(It was odd, this not-having-a-body, not being seen – it meant you saw the things that happened behind your back, you saw the things people didn't know they were showing.)

"Oh! I'll ask him," said Sam, finally looking up and wiping tears of laughter away.

Katt's face snapped back into a wide smile.

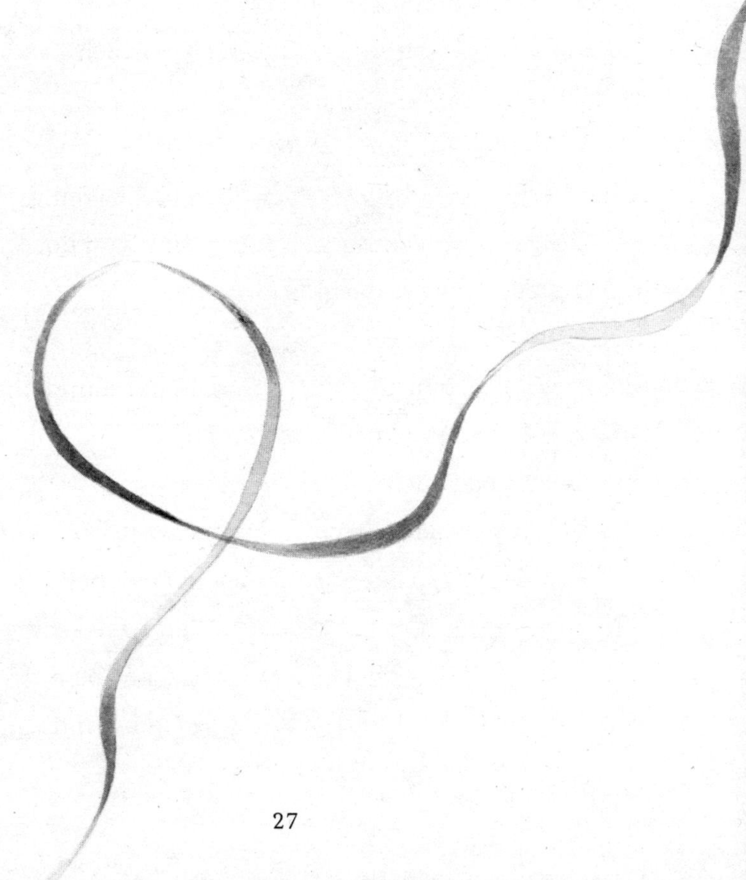

EIGHT

THORN LOOKED AT her body's face. She never saw it usually. Never knew what it looked like anywhere other than in the occasional mirror when it knew it was being looked at.

It had stopped laughing now, was half looking out the window, half throwing comments back at the other girls, as the hubbub of people shifting and chatting and farting and stretching went on all around them.

Her face looked odd. Ugly? No. Not quite. Not really.

Unfamiliar, maybe, this way round.

Her eyes were too dark, her chin too small. Her cheeks weren't smooth and unblemished like the magazines and she had a habit of popping her tongue out between her front teeth, just the tip of it, when she was absent-mindedly doing nothing.

(Just any girl's face, really.)

But as she watched it, and listened to the words that came out of its mouth, Thorn was amazed.

The words just appeared, one after the other. Words, then words, then words.

When she was in her body, indeed even now while she *wasn't* in her body, words were so hard to come by.

No, that wasn't true.

The inside of her skull spun with them, was full of them; circling and looping endlessly round inside her head, nosily practising themselves, forming themselves, testing themselves, repeating themselves – waiting for the right lull in a conversation to step out into the world.

And half the time, more than half the time, the words never got the chance to get out, and those little loops of thought just withered on the vine and were never shared, like . . . what? What was it that withered on vines? Grapes? Apples? Bananas?

No, she thought, *not bananas. I don't think they grow on vines. I've an idea they grow in bushes, pointing up. They call them 'hands', don't they? Is a bunch of bananas called a 'hand'? And they come in boats, boxes of bunches of bananas on boats with tarantulas hiding in them that bite dockworkers. And the boats come from . . . oh, where? From the Caribbean, or from South America? Somewhere like that. Distant, sunny places. Certainly not from here, or from the Nextdoor Country.*

And, as she thought all that and was glad she had no one to say it all to, because she didn't want them to think her odd (or odd*er*), Mr Crookhey called the register and everyone streamed out and off to their first lessons of the day.

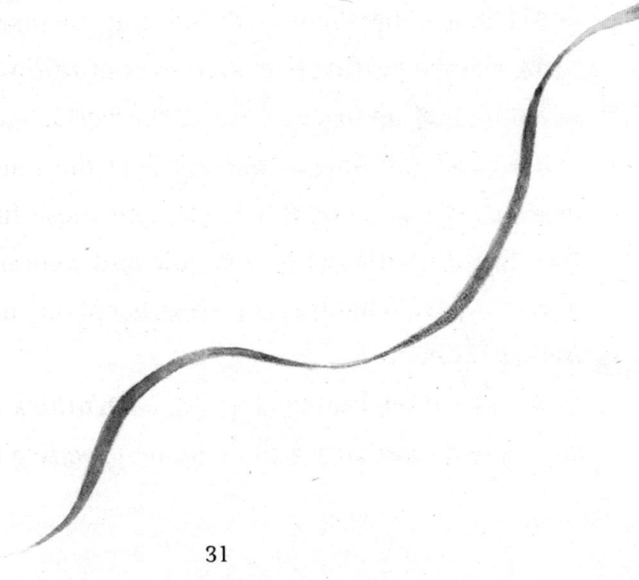

NINE

THORN JUST STAYED there and watched them all go.

She couldn't bring herself to push into or through that mass of bodies cramming through the door.

She'd catch up.

The feeling that they were person-shaped clockwork machines had, in that moment as they'd all suddenly moved, heaving and pushing and jostling, bumping up against each other, so physical, solid and yielding, filled her up. They were just automata that someone had wound up and set going, just following the directions of their cogs and gears and springs.

All the years she'd spent in her body she'd believed, without ever really thinking about it, that everyone was

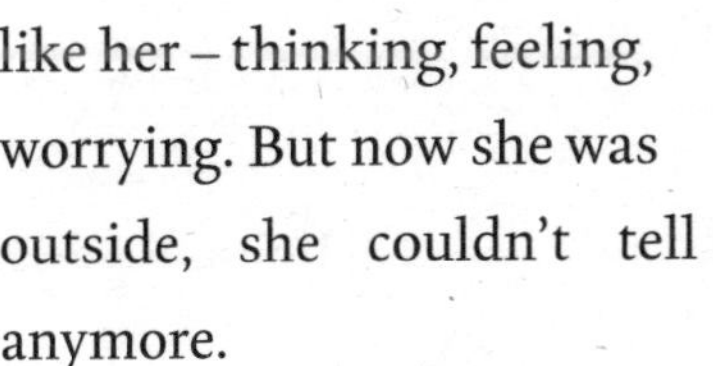

like her – thinking, feeling, worrying. But now she was outside, she couldn't tell anymore.

They hadn't changed. But seeing her own body getting on fine without her in it was making her think. (What else could she do, but think?)

Seeing it say the things she would've said in the conversation with Sam and Katt, she'd realised they could've just been the programmed responses of a computer, and no one would've been able to tell the difference.

She couldn't.

"What about me?" asked the window she was staring out. "How do you think I feel?"

"It's clear what you feel," said Thorn.

"Transparently so," said the window.

While she was outside her body, Thorn thought, why shouldn't the world talk?

Windows and alarm clocks and car radios were just as much real things as the meat-machine teenagers jam-packing the corridors. And just because she had never thought they thought, never thought that things in the world might have an inner life, an 'interior monologue' as her English teacher would say, didn't mean they didn't or couldn't or shouldn't.

From outside, how could you tell the difference between thinking, living things, and the rest of the stuff?

What if it was *all* (both objects *and* people) just 'the-rest-of-the-stuff', inanimate matter pretending to be living?

Argh! Stop thinking! she thought, feeling fizzy with all the dizzying ideas. *Just stop it!*

Too much!

Too much!

Thursday wasn't a day for philosophy lessons.

It was time for Maths.

TEN

"WAKE UP!" SHOUTED the desks. "Get off me!"

They groaned under the weight of the leaning teenagers draped across their polished tops like lounging antelopes, all dangling limbs and yawning heads.

All the students' energy had evaporated in the Maths room.

Thorn looked around for her body and saw it was over near the back, which wasn't a surprise. It knew exactly how to be her. That was where she always sat.

Katt and Sam had gone off to different classes, so she was sat next to a too-tall boy she didn't much like called Clive.

Clive's shirt stretched at the neck and his tie was too short. His hair pointed in two different directions and his hands were already covered with ink stains.

"Morning," he said to her body.

"Morning," her body said to him.

And then Thorn noticed something odd happen.

The cheeks of her body flushed, and it looked away, reached down, fiddled in its pencil case.

Her body was embarrassed.

It had said one word to Clive, this gangly lad she sat beside every Maths class only because her friends weren't around, and she'd blushed and looked away.

Her body *fancied* Clive.

Clive!

Gods!

And then something even odder happened.

Thorn remembered.

There, drifting above the scene, she *remembered.*

She remembered two things.

Firstly, she remembered this day. It had happened before, but the first time round she'd been inside her body, in her brain, thinking and feeling and living it. Treading water, breathing air, keeping going.

And secondly she remembered what had happened the night before this day.

She'd had a dream.

It had been such an odd dream, deep and strong and powerful, and even though she couldn't remember the details (neither now, nor when she'd lived this day) she knew, in the guts she didn't have, the dagger-in-the-heart, bullseye certainty with which she'd woken up: she'd fallen for Clive.

Clive!

Something had hooked her heart. Even though she'd never had a crush before, and even though the conversations some of the girls had left her numb with embarrassment and wordless with lack of experience, she'd woken up that morning knowing, in her heart of hearts, that Clive was the one for her.

How daft!

Watching the scene from above, from outside, watching her body fumble for words to say, Thorn laughed.

And, from the new vantage point she had, she watched Clive's face, and it was 1000% clear he hadn't the foggiest clue about the turmoil and knots and loopy handwritten thoughts (loopy, with hearts drawn in place of the dots of the 'i's) going on in the thing beside him.

His face was blank and yawning and ignoring Mr Pascal, who had started talking about numbers or something.

"Ooh, that tickles," said the board, as the marker pen began squeaking across it.

ELEVEN

IF THIS WAS a day that she *remembered*, a day that had *already* happened, then that must mean she was dreaming it now, dreaming the day again. Surely that was the answer?

This was just a dream-memory that she'd become lost in, or stuck in somehow.

But she'd never heard of that happening to anyone before.

Then again, maybe that was just because no one talked about it, since talking about getting stuck inside a dream was the sort of thing doctors would lock you up for.

But that didn't happen, either, not in real life. Doctors in white coats didn't turn up and bundle people into padded vans. She knew enough to know that if you had mental health problems, like she might be having, it took months for anyone to take notice and months longer for help to be got, if help was available at all.

Gods, she thought. *That's bleak.*

But it wasn't a perfect world.

It wasn't a helpful or caring world a lot of the time.

Thorn looked back at her body.

It was chewing the end of its pen, and looking at Clive's hand on the desk – playing with the edge of his textbook, curling the corner and letting it flick back – while not looking like it was looking.

(She knew there were organs pumping and gurgling inside it, doing all those things animal bodies do in order to stay warm, to stay alive. Never still, never silent. *Gurgle, gurgle, gurgle.* The same thing was happening in every person in the room; a forest of pulsating meat. It was revolting to think about, she thought. But maybe it was those chemicals and hormones and fluids inside you that gave you the feelings – the adrenalin surge of fear, the endolphins (was that the word?) of happiness . . . maybe, she thought, that explained why she was taking all this in her stride, instead of freaking out?)

Thorn's body's face was blank and simple. It wasn't trying

to convey any meaning, just being flat and unobserved as it watched Clive's fingers.

Except it wasn't unobserved.

Thorn was observing it, and, she noticed, from across the room someone else was observing it too.

TWELVE

MEADOWBLOSSOM WAS A girl with long blond hair rolling onto her shoulders. It always looked as if a gentle breeze was running its fingers through it. Thorn had vaguely known her for years, but had never taken any notice.

They'd never been friends, never enemies.

Meadowblossom was one of those kids who'd arrived as refugees, years and years ago, from the Nextdoor Country. Something had happened there that had made it unsafe for her family. Something unsafe was always happening there.

She spoke with a soft accent, smoothed over by years of growing up here.

Her father's accent, when he called to her across the street, was sour and strong.

There must be an age after which, no matter how long you live in another country, your accent won't change, Thorn thought.

In her head she tried it on, but she'd never been a good mimic.

Right now, in this Maths class that Thorn was remembering or dreaming (a Maths class that must be in her past, which raised the question of 'When exactly is *now*, then?'), Meadowblossom was staring at her body.

Freed from being in her body, Thorn was able to notice things she'd not seen the first time round, and that look of Meadowblossom's was one of them.

She was looking at Thorn's body in the same way that Thorn's body was looking at Clive.

How had she never noticed?

Was today the only day or the first day or the latest day Meadowblossom had looked at her that way? Or had she stared like that – shyly, nervously, hungrily – every day?

Thorn was embarrassed.

She was glad she'd never noticed.

Meadowblossom was one of those freaks from over there.

(*That's unfair*, she thought.)

She was sad she'd never noticed.

Meadowblossom had never done her any harm.

As Thorn remembered the feeling of fancying Clive, of waking from that morning's dream consumed with the thought of him, owned by it, warm with it, so, she imagined, Meadowblossom was thinking of her.

And her body was totally clueless.

And Gods, this fancying stuff was weird. She didn't know how to feel about it, not really. She'd never thought about a girlfriend, had barely even thought about a boyfriend – but the idea, the realisation, the knowledge, that someone (anyone!) was actually thinking about her . . . Well, that was stunning.

But she knows nothing of me, Thorn thought. *She doesn't know me at all. All she knows is the body, what it looks like, what it does and says, but she can't know me.* By that she meant the part that was thinking, that was observing here and now, the part that made the decisions, that had the feelings, that thought the things the body didn't say.

I think things I never say, she thought. *No one knows that.*

What was stunning, it became apparent to her, was the realisation that Meadowblossom (and Clive and Sam and Katt and her brother Gregor) must also think things they never said, never shared, that whole silent worlds happened in their skulls.

(Also: *I say things I don't mean. I say 'I'm fine' when I'm not, and I bet everyone else does too. You don't know their secret worlds, and you can't trust what they say!* Being human was suddenly very difficult.)

But right now, more importantly, there was an idea of Thorn, a version of Thorn, existing inside that other girl's head.

A me, Thorn thought, *that I am not responsible for, that I have no control over. It might say or do anything in her head. Just as I have an idea of who she is, who Clive is, who Gregor is that exists only in my skull (not that I'm in my skull right now).*

Gods!

She couldn't remember thinking so hard before.

Mr Pascal droned on about Maths.

Clive continued flicking his pages.

Thorn's body continued doing whatever it was doing.

And Meadowblossom chewed her thumbnail and continued to stare across the room, eyes partially shaded by her ever-swaying hair.

Thorn turned away.

She needed time away from all this (sitting down, not doing anything much) activity.

THIRTEEN

OUT IN THE corridor there was something close to silence.

Only the rows of closed doors murmured, whisperingly, across the grey lino.

Thorn looked around.

Everything was so familiar. The posters, the room numbers, the scuff marks on the flooring.

How often had she walked this corridor in her waking life? And now she was drifting along it, pushed by her will, forwards, backwards, left, right – a floating point of view.

A new thought arose – floating, drifting, waking . . . sleeping . . .

When you went into hospital, she thought, to have a big

operation, they gave you drugs to put you to sleep. Maybe she was lying on an operating table now, stoned out of her mind on anaesthetic, and was dream-remembering this day.

What was wrong with her?

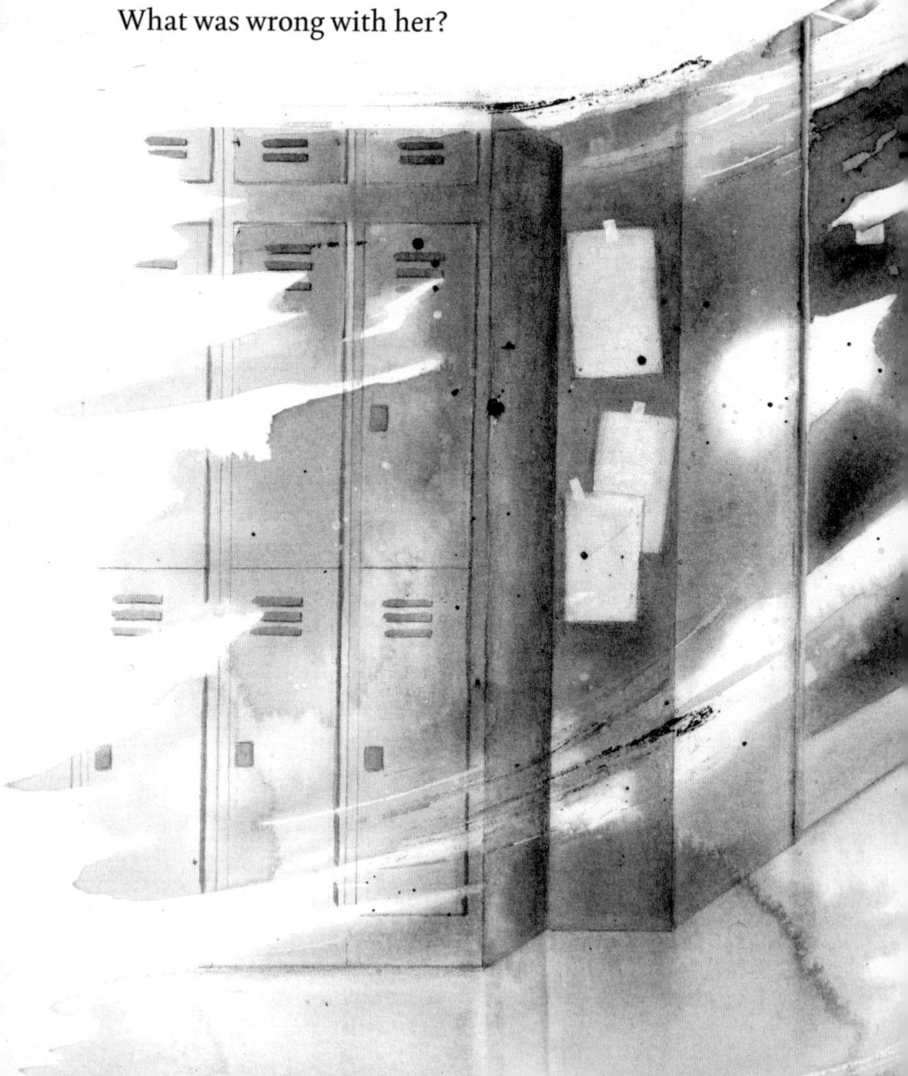

What had happened?

You didn't end up in hospital for nothing. You only went there at those life-changing, life-saving times – when you needed the doctor's special skills, the surgeon's skills.

What happened to me?

Suddenly something passed by the place where her ankles would have been, had she had ankles.

The movement caught her eye and she looked down.

There was a cat.

A scruffy, mangy old thing, with a bent tail and odd-coloured eyes.

It padded under her and trotted along the corridor, towards where the stairs led back to the ground floor.

"Hello?" said Thorn, feeling slightly silly even as she said it.

So many things had spoken to her today, she wouldn't have been surprised if the cat had turned around and looked up at her and spoken too.

I mean, if anything could see me, it'd be a cat.

But the cat didn't turn, it just padded away, tail raised, bum winking, smell lingering.

And then, beyond it, at the end of the corridor, where it

split at a T-junction and two staircases led down, a figure appeared.

It stepped strangely, tentatively, queerly, from around the corner, tiptoeing on long pointed shoes across the junction, across the space that led from one staircase to the other.

There should've been wonky accordion music playing, but there wasn't.

The figure was dressed in garish red and blue and yellow clothes, tight in places, puffy and loose in others. Its nose was long – not *big* but long – and the eye that Thorn could see sparkled like a tropical ocean, blue as an egg.

It its white-gloved hands it held an oversized pair of scissors, with blades sharp and silver and shining.

Tiptoe.

Tiptoe.

Tiptoe.

Those extra-long legs, pantomiming, reaching out like a praying mantis with each step, finding the exact spot to land, and then pausing before touching down.

Pausing at odd moments along the way, too, between movements, out of synch with nature.

Unnatural clockwork.

Stop motion.

Stop.   Motion.   Stop.

And it grinned. Was grinning. Its face didn't change, it remained side on to her, always side on, in profile, that one blue eye swiveling around.

She suddenly remembered, all in a flash, a Punch and Judy show she'd seen when she was little. They'd been at the seaside, on holiday, and she and Gregor had been left on the sand before the striped tent. She hadn't known what to expect and when the puppets had appeared, shouting with their high scrapy voices, she'd screamed.

Gregor never let her forget.

They came from over there, the Nextdoor Country, he said. That was why they were so creepy, but he'd not been scared and had thrown pebbles at the tent until he was forced to leave and take his bawling little sister with him.

He loved that story.

This stranger in her school reminded her of Mr Punch. Not exactly the same, but close enough – something like a puppet, but not quite. Just odd. Artificial. Peculiar.

The cat, which had been trotting happily towards that

end of the corridor, turned a smooth circle, and, without running, padded back past Thorn in the opposite direction.

No rush.

Thorn didn't feel *afraid* exactly, but she felt deep down in every fibre of whatever she was, that she *ought* to be, deeply.

And the too-tall man with the scissors suddenly paused, midway across the stairwell, one long foot in the air, and, before he could turn, step closer and properly look at her, Thorn hurried back into the classroom.

FOURTEEN

OH?

That rush of memory, that flash of childhood, must've confused her, sent her wrong.

Thorn had definitely gone through the Maths door, but she'd not ended up in the Maths classroom.

For a moment, as she took it in, she thought she'd somehow ended up in the Art department, but then she realised this wasn't one of those rooms either.

It was a largish, black-floored, white-walled space, with paintings hanging here and there, like they were on display.

In one corner a grey metal, spider-like sculpture stood, gently waving its little bits and pieces, back and forth, back and forth. Across from that a blue dress was shredded in ribbons and pinned to the wall, splayed like spaghetti.

Modern art.

In front of the largest painting was a pair of people. They were adults, maybe teachers.

But then, no, they weren't teachers, and she wasn't in school.

One was her mother.

And one was her brother.

Except . . . her brother looked older.

She'd seen him not much more than an hour before, at breakfast, and he'd looked exactly like himself – but here, in front of her now, he looked like a grown up, like a man.

Gregor's hair was trimmed short, and his stubble was trimmed short, and his sense of patience was trimmed short.

"Come on, let's go," he said.

Where am I? Thorn thought.

Her mum sighed.

She held her hand up to point at the painting.

"I wonder, what's it meant to be?" she said. "It's very odd, isn't it?"

"Come on," said Gregor. "I'm on duty in an hour. We came, we looked, we went."

"I don't think I really get it. Why does it have to be so ugly?"

Thorn went over to them and looked at what they were looking at (or what they weren't really looking at).

This was an art gallery, clearly, and they were not art lovers.

It was all most puzzling.

The painting was large, and strange.

There was a broken, muddy, wet landscape, a dark landscape, with floating, ghostlike figures passing over it. There were mechanical objects, things, machines – spindly, fragile and not obviously for doing anything, besides being a part of this artist's landscape. And there, in the top left corner, was a flash of colour, a bright spot in the gloom – a blue-orange blur, darting away.

Oh! Thorn knew what that was. Although it was only a blur, she felt certain it was a kingfisher. That bird, again!

It was an incongruous splash of light, swimming against the grey flow of the other figures, the ghost figures, who were moving, or being drawn, the other way, into the path of the machines.

She wanted to ask what it all meant, but the world was being quiet.

And when she turned around she saw that her mum and her brother had gone.

For a moment Thorn was alone, and then she wasn't.

She saw there were other people around, maybe they'd been there all along, in couples or in trios, looking at the art. They commented in hushed whispers about this or that painting or sculpture or assemblage of things. They were students maybe, in their twenties, dressed smart scruffy, mixed with a few older adults, dressed smart smart. They seemed to smile and laugh quietly.

And then a tall young man rushed into the white space of the gallery, stepped in from somewhere, came to stop almost exactly in Thorn's hovering point of view. (She shifted herself to the side.) He flicked his floppy hair out of his eyes and scratched at his scraggly goatee beard with long fingers.

And he was joined, from the opposite end of the gallery, by a young woman.

They met in front of the painting.

There was something about them she thought she knew, that rang the tiniest of bells, far off. But she couldn't think where she might've seen them before.

"They've gone," the young woman said.

"Yeah," the young man replied. "I passed them as I came in."

"It was good of them to stay so long," the young woman said, with what Thorn thought was sarcasm.

"Did you talk to them?"

"No."

What the hell's going on? she thought. *I was in school, and now, all of a sudden, I'm here, wherever here is. With these people, whoever they are . . . It doesn't make any sense.*

And then she thought, *I'll go. I'll move myself outside and find my way to somewhere I know.*

But she didn't.

She just stayed there and looked at that strange painting, filled as it was with crumbling pain. Those spirits, those ghosts, she saw as she looked closer, were all nailed to the ground, iron spikes driven into their trailing spirit-sheets.

And yet, there was something in it, in that bird in the corner, that called to her.

"Do you want a drink?" the man said, as the pair walked away from the painting.

"No," said the woman. "She gets off duty at nine. I'm going to go meet her."

"Oh, OK."

"I'll make you tea, though. There's a kettle in the office. There's time for that."

And they left, out into the backroom, and Thorn thought, *OK, enough.*

"Is anything going to talk to me?" she shouted. And when no one turned around and the world remained silent, she said, "OK, I'm going to find something that will."

And she pushed herself off from the wall, and drifted over to the front doors, hoping to maybe see that cat again, or to get back to her friends, or back to her body . . .

But as she passed through the doors, as she moved into darkness, into the nighttime outside, she was ambushed by a violent, shrieking blare of horns, and a blast of light, and she spun, her senses momentarily, shockingly, overwhelmed.

FIFTEEN

WHEN SHE REGAINED her senses, Thorn realised that she wasn't in the street and she wasn't back in the Maths room or in the corridor or at home.

She was somewhere else entirely.

Somewhere explodingly loud.

At first she couldn't understand it, but her senses slowly, slowly sorted themselves out, lined the world up in order again.

The noise clanged and echoed around her, made of shrieks and whistles, crashes and splashes.

The smell was chemical, familiar.

The light, bright and high up.

The space was huge.

This was the central swimming pool, in town.

A whistle blew, suddenly, right beside her.

There was a man there, dressed in shorts and a T-shirt, with a big brown moustache on his face and a huge watch on his wrist.

Oh, Thorn thought. *I remember him.*

"It's time," said the huge watch. "Swap 'em over, Bob. Quick. Quick!"

The man, Bob, nodded and blew his whistle again.

"Everyone out!" he shouted, even as the sharp stab of sound *echo-echo-echo*ed round the pool.

She hadn't known him as Bob. To her he'd been Mr Williamson.

Thorn hadn't seen him for years.

A group of little kids, seven- or eight-year-olds maybe, crocodiled out of the changing rooms onto the pool edge. They gossiped and chattered as they came, their little tight swimming caps a rainbow forest of bobbing mushrooms.

And, at the same time, the kids in the pool began climbing out, over in the corner where there was a metal ladder. She saw them swimming towards it and clustering like fishes round a . . . well, whatever it was that fishes clustered round.

A hook? A net? A dead body?

Except.

Except, that wasn't all that was happening.

One little girl had stepped away from the class lining up by the wall, waiting for their turn in the pool, and had got closer to the water.

"Thorn," hissed a child's voice. "Come back."

And Thorn suddenly understood this wasn't any random little girl – it was her, or, to be precise, her body. But it wasn't the teenage body she was used to, this was happening years before, with her primary-school class, at the pool for a swimming lesson.

Thorn looked at her body, at its nose, its hair poking out from under her cap. Her thin chest. Her big feet. They looked like those of a duck. Had she really looked like that once? She would grow into her feet, she'd catch them up. She knew that now, and she wished she could say it to her body here. She remembered the moments of self-consciousness, of shyness.

"*Miss! Miss! Thorn's going quackers!*"

But her body wasn't having one of those self-conscious moments now.

Shyness was not on today's menu.

It was shouting from the edge of the water, little wavelets washing over the tiles, chlorine-ing her toes.

"Hey! Gregor! Hey! Hi!"

Her body was looking at someone, one of the swimming caps in the pool.

She was calling to her brother.

And Thorn had a sudden memory.

And Thorn had a sudden foreboding.

And Thorn had a sudden unlocking.

She knew what was going to happen.

"Shut up!" she shouted, uselessly. "Leave him alone! Let him be!"

But Gregor, her older brother, had changed course, out in the ocean depths.

He was swimming towards her.

Bob, Mr Williamson, had wandered off and Thorn floated in front of her old classmates, watching her body waving.

Her brother was ploughing through the water towards them.

He was a good, strong swimmer.

He had shoulders made for it.

He didn't mind putting his head under the water.

His hands were slightly webbed.

(That last one wasn't true, but it was something of a family joke. They said it with love, and Gregor didn't really mind it. Some untrue things are like that.)

As he swam, behind him, in the deeps, sharks rose up.

Grey fins broke the surface of the water, with a frothing fringe of white foam.

They followed, getting closer.

But, Thorn thought, it hadn't been like this. They hadn't been sharks, not in the pool. Of course they hadn't.

"Oh, but they were," said a voice from down on the tiles.

She looked.

There was the cat from the corridor, rocked back on its spine, licking its unmentionables. Its odd-coloured eyes twinkled in the bright high halogen lamplight.

"What?" she said.

"They were always sharks," it said. "Always will be. Deep down."

"They were bullies," she said. "Just bums-for-brains."

(Why that phrase? She must've be channelling the little Thorn bouncing on her toes at the poolside.)

"Potato, potato," the cat said, pronouncing both words the same way.

"Sharks," she muttered under her breath.

Gregor had almost reached the side of the pool now, his fingertips about to slap tile.

Her body, still waving, smiling, laughing. (She had *liked* her brother, once. They'd been pals and chums and he'd played games with her, before they'd both grown up.) It stepped back, to be among her classmates, to be away from the splashing water.

The sharks were closing, and now she saw the fins had gone, they were just the outlines of boys from his class, torpedoing under the surface.

And as Gregor got his elbows on the edge, and thrust himself up, hauled himself up, levered himself up, the sharks' fingers snagged his shorts, his swimming shorts, and he pulled himself into the poolside air stark naked.

For a moment there was silence.

Gregor hadn't realised what had happened.

He broke the silence by saying, "Hey, Thorn! All OK?"

Thorn's body turned red, stuttered, spluttered, pointed and implored him with its eyes to pull his pants back up.

And then her whole class burst into laughter.

Boys and girls, screaming, pointing.

Some turned away.

Some stared.

Gregor's hairless little winkle twinkled in the bright lights.

And then he realised.

And, even though she herself was free of the chemicals that caused such things, Thorn knew the emotions surging through him – shame, embarrassment, anger.

They radiated like radio waves.

And from the water the sharks roared, toothy, bloody battle-cries of wicked joy.

And beside her body she heard words come from the mouths of a pair of kids she'd forgotten had been there.

Meadowblossom and Honeysweet. The refugee kids.

"Nasty ——," they said.

"Dirty ——," they said.

Neither Thorn nor her body knew what the second word was. It was in that difficult whispered language they'd brought with them, but from where they were pointing, and the pinched, wicked looks on their faces, they both understood enough.

As the moment unfroze, Gregor slapped his hands down to cover his dignity, to protect his modesty, and at the same time he turned away. (The natural human instinct is, for whatever reason, that buttocks are less rude than the full-frontal slideshow.) But his swimming shorts were down around his ankles, and as he turned he tangled, and as he tangled he toppled.

He fall awkwardly on the tiles, banging something, cracking something, and rolling into the water.

But Thorn's body didn't notice this, because it was busy punching Meadowblossom in the nose and pulling Honeysweet by the hair.

(Why hadn't she remembered this, earlier? Why hadn't she remembered this incident, when she'd looked at Meadowblossom in Maths?)

"Leave my brother alone!" her body shouted.

"Don't you dare!" her body roared.

"Monsters!" her body yelled.

And, of course, the day collapsed into chaos, and swimming was cancelled, and her body had to go sit outside the Head's office, and her brother was taken to hospital to be checked over (it was actually the sharks who had saved him, and hauled him out of the pool), and everyone just felt awful . . .

And Thorn was left at the side of the pool remembering it all again.

SIXTEEN

"WHAT'S GOING ON with me?" she said.

"That's what I wondered," said the cat.

"How come I'm here?"

"I wondered that too."

"I mean, my body's gone off, back to school. If this is a memory, how come I'm still here, when I can't possibly remember this bit?"

"Is this what memories are like?" the cat asked.

Thorn thought about it.

The cat padded along the poolside, glancing into the water, not caring that its paws were getting wet.

"No," she said. "Memories are just ideas in your head. This is different. I'm actually here. I was actually in the school, at that art show. I was watching it all happen. That's not how memories work at all."

And then she realised the swimming pool had fallen silent around them, or almost silent. Only the gentle *slap slap slap* of soft, washing waves sounded.

And the cat paused, glanced over its shoulder at her, turned back to the pool and, in a sudden darting punch, speared a small fish on its clawed paw. It dragged it out onto the tiles and crunched its head.

After a moment it said, "It's all memory, really, the whole of life – but you're skipping."

"What?"

"Skipping in time. You've become a little unstuck, that's all. It probably won't last long and soon everything will be back to normal. You'll be found, stuck back in place."

"What? What do you mean?"

"You've seen the solution, but you ran away."

Thorn thought.

"Oh," she said, thinking she realised what the cat meant. She hovered above it.

After a moment she said, "How come you can see me?"

"Oh, I'm a cat," said the cat. "Your cat."

The school bell rang.

It sounded like an explosion.

Light, darkness, crashing.

Thorn spun around and was in that long stale corridor of familiar doors once again.

SEVENTEEN

STUDENTS RUSHED THIS way and that, a roar of banging bags and loud whispering voices and knotty jostling.

Thorn looked around and saw Clive's tall head bobbing away from her.

It took her a few long seconds of searching before she saw her own body trailing along behind him in the crowd. It looked just like all the other bodies.

She was faintly disappointed that she hadn't felt any instant recognition, any sense of ownership from across the corridor. It didn't feel right that her body was just like all the others. She wondered about the last time she'd been in it, looking out of its eyes, hearing with its ears (and although she couldn't remember exactly *when* or *where* that had been, she could remember *what* it was like) – it had been the whole world to her. She had been the centre of the world. Of her world. (The only world.) Things were measured by their distance from her, people by their relation to her.

Thorn had never existed in a place where she wasn't at the centre, wasn't present.

Now though . . .

Now it was different.

Her body was just one body among hundreds, lost in the crowd.

(If she'd been in her body the thought would've made her feel sick.)

No, not lost in the crowd. There it was – trailing behind Clive, whose head she could still see, and they were heading into a classroom.

It was a different day to where she'd started this morning, she realised, as she followed them into the Biology lab. No Biology on Thursdays. Not in the same week as double Maths, anyway.

"Settle down, everyone," said Miss Passell, the teacher. "Settle down."

Chairs scraped.

Desks banged.

Uniforms sighed.

Bodies slumped to attention.

Thorn floated in the background.

Her body was sat on a stool next to Clive, but the way it looked lacked the intense tension of earlier.

This is definitely another day, she thought. *Another day.*

And she suddenly remembered that that pash of hers, that crush, had only lasted a few days, the fading hangover from that vivid Wednesday night dream. She remembered waking up on the Monday, expecting to be going back to school on another buzzing, 'maybe-he'll-notice-me-*today*' day, and realising that, actually, she didn't care any more.

It had been odd and funny (feelings were so odd and funny – out of your control and yet telling you this, telling you that), and she'd laughed and shaken her head and blushed to herself, and had been so incredibly thankful she'd not told anyone how she'd been feeling. Not Sam, not Katt, definitely not Clive. No one ever, and now her secret was forever safe and gossipless.

This was maybe whole weeks later. Months, even.

Here, in the lab, she was endlessly reminded of what bodies were. The charts on the walls showed her the facts. The textbooks stacked in the cupboard sang the truth.

Bodies are biological machines filled with fluids and chemicals and pumps and organs, that move around and make noises and bump into things and bruise and bleed and hurt and ache. And it's those fluids and chemicals, adrenaline and endorphins (that's the word!) and so on, getting in the brain, in the stomach, in the kidneys and the elsewheres, that create all these feelings, and sweats and spots and crazy moments of . . .

Oh, she thought, *some love chemicals in my brain got unbalanced by my dream and made me think I fancied Clive! And then they drained away and I went back to normal. Bodies are so daft!*

Ah, she also thought again, reaffirming her earlier suspicions here, surrounded by the confirming charts and posters, *I don't have any chemicals at all now, so that's why I'm fearless.*

EIGHTEEN

MISS PASSELL WADDLED to the front of the room. She was pregnant and had been for ages.

At first it was an embarrassment. The boys in particular didn't know where to look. (It was bad enough seeing a teacher in town, or in the supermarket, but seeing the evidence that they'd . . . *done it* . . . that was even worse, it seemed.) But now it was just how she was. Round and loud and red.

She had a large brown paper bag on her desk.

There were damp patches round the bottom, at the corners.

"Today," she said, "you need to get your dissection kits out. We've had a special delivery."

Thorn looked around the room.

That explained why Meadowblossom wasn't here. They were in the same set for Biology, but being from the Nextdoor Country she was excused dissection. It was something against their culture, and we had to be respectful of their culture. That's what they always said, even though the programmes on the telly made jokes out of it all the time.

On the windowsill behind Miss Passell the cactuses (cacti?) sang softly to themselves in the sunlight that poured through the glass, even as raindrops spattered it. They seemed so happy, just being spiky and sunny and green.

"OK, it's time to look inside the eye."

Miss Passell lifted a lightly leaking plastic box out of the paper bag, and plonked it down, heavily, on her desk.

Eyeballs.

A tub full of eyeballs.

She squelched the cover off and passed the box to the kids sat in front of her.

"Take one and pass them on. One eye between two," she said.

There were gasps and complaints, damp hands were wiped on trousers and jumpers, but the tub was passed on, and eyeballs were plopped down on the desks in front of each pair.

"Now, what is an animal?" Miss Passell said.

Hands went up.

"Thorn?"

Thorn said, "Pardon?"

She hadn't put her hand up, not having a hand, and she hadn't expected to be picked.

"A tube," said her body.

Oh, she thought, *I'd forgotten about her.*

"That's right," said Miss Passell. "A tube with . . ."

"Elaborations," said Thorn's body along with several other pupils.

They half-sang the word.

Thorn didn't remember this particular lesson (maybe it hadn't happened yet, maybe this was her future?), but she recognised the answer. It was one of the things Miss Passell had said more than once.

"An animal," she would say, "including you lot, including me, is just a tube with a mouth at one end and an anus at the other." (Usually some boys sniggered at that.) "A self-sustaining tube that passes other bits of the world through it in order to extract enough energy to allow it to keep on tubing, and to make more tubes. Baby tubes. To perpetuate its tubiness. And millions of years of evolution have given the tube all sorts of elaborations to make it more efficient at being self-sustaining. Such as . . . ?"

Hands would go up.

"Teeth," someone would say.

"Yes. They give the tube a head start on digesting food. Break it up small. What else?"

"Lungs."

"Yes. They provide another source of energy, to help digest the food."

"Legs?"

"Yes. If a tube can move about, it'll find more food."

"Flippers! Fins!"

"Opposable thumbs."

"Eyes."

"Yes. Yes. Yes. Eyes, and the other sense organs, make a tube better at finding food. And there are all the other things we've evolved or invented, even things beyond the body: love," (*giggles*), "sex," (*more giggles*), "religion," (*stifled gasps*), "parliamentary democracy," (*silence*), "music," (*more silence*), "art," (*yawns*). "They're all things tubes have made to make being a tube bearable." She paused. Took a deep breath. Took a sip of coffee. "And now let's see how the eye itself works . . ."

And so she began showing them what was what, and where to cut on the little tight leathery sacks of jelly before them.

Thorn looked at her body.

She and Clive were leaning over their eyeball.

It had a rectangular pupil. A dark slot-like slit.

"I think it's a goat," said Clive.

"How can you tell?" said Thorn's body.

"Because that's the shape of a goat's pupil," Thorn and Clive said at the same time.

"No other animal's got one like that," he continued.

"Oh," said Thorn's body. "That's weird."

How did Thorn know that and her body didn't? That didn't seem right.

Maybe this wasn't her future then. If this was the time her body learnt the shape of a goat's pupil, then this must be her past as well . . .

The me of the me of me's from after this time, she thought.

"Have you ever seen a cuttlefish's eye?" Clive asked.

"Isn't that a squid thing?"

"Yeah."

Thorn knew what was coming next.

"Their pupils are shaped like Ws. Sort of zigzaggy."

It was true. Thorn remembered seeing them somewhere. Maybe on telly. Maybe in an aquarium.

"No!" said her body. "What *really*?"

In her body's hand the eyeball was looking around.

While they were busy talking about other eyes, this one was staring at the desktop, staring at the scalpel that was lingering just in its field of vision.

Thorn watched as green grass tufted up from the wooden surface, from the floor around the desks.

The classroom was filling with grass. Deep, rich meadow grass, with little yellow and white and blue flowers and butterflies.

The sunshine shone and somewhere a blackbird sang a long line of liquid song.

And then, from the riverbank behind Clive and her body, an emerald-blue lozenge of light burst up, straight up out of the grass there. But it wasn't made of light, it was made of flesh and bone and feather and dream, and it was a shining kingfisher.

It arced across the room and landed on the window-handle above the cacti (cactuses?), preened under one wing, then tapped on the glass with its dagger beak, saying, "Out, please! Out now! Out!"

And Miss Passell reached up, without really looking, and opened the fanlight with one hand, and the bird, flapped up, circled tightly, dove out the gap, and vanished off out into the wide sunlit world, and behind it, in the classroom, in the Biology lab, the grass fell away and Thorn's body let out a yelp and a gurgle and a shriek and Thorn spun round.

NINETEEN

WHAT HAD HAPPENED was clear.

Thorn's body had been pressing down with its scalpel on the tough outer layer of her goat eye, feeling the resistance, feeling the toughness, and then . . . Oh, then! The knife had found the right angle, the sweet spot, and had plunged in, uncontrolled, and the vitreous humour had squirted.

Oh, gods!

It suddenly came back to her.

She'd been so distracted, had had her mind filled with so many other things, that she'd forgotten what was about to happen to her body.

But suddenly, as she watched it fall from the stool, she

remembered the way the fluid – the liquid in the eyeball that had belonged to an elaboration of a tube which was actually an animal called a goat, once alive, now dead – had sprayed as her blade had slipped, and squirted into her eyes and up her nose. It had been vaguely warm, clammily cold, totally disgusting.

An invasion of her personal space. Of her personal face.

She'd huffed and spat and cried, not sadly or weakly, but she'd been a slave to her body's automatic responses against invasion, against foreign matter getting on her private surfaces – *Kick it out! Wash it away!*

But seeing the scene from the outside she thought, *Gods, she's making such a fuss. It was only a little vitreous humour, which is 98% water. What a silly so-and-so!*

And then she thought, *But it felt so much worse. I couldn't see! I couldn't breathe!*

And then she thought, *Look at Clive!*

From her free-floating point of view she saw something she hadn't seen at the time.

The gangly boy was crouched over her, a hand hovering above her shoulder, not quite touching, pulling tissues out of his pocket, while the other kids were coming over,

laughing, crowding, muttering. And the look on Clive's face was that of a great worried puppy.

His eyes, unlike that of the goat, were thrumming with life, with future, with hope.

But as her body calmed, wiped its face, snorted its snot, shook its head, Clive's face returned to normal.

They might just be tubes of meat that have evolved to be self-sustaining, Thorn thought, but there's all sorts going on inside.

I don't know, can't know, what he's thinking, or what he's feeling, she thought, *but I* think *I know,*

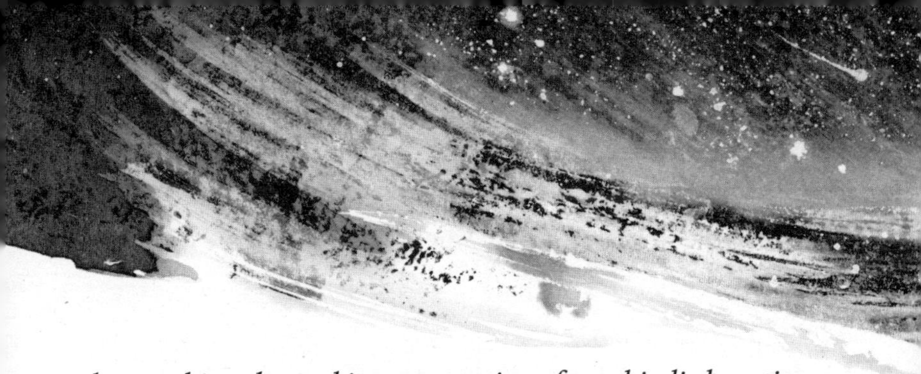

by watching, by making assumptions from his little actions. But I look at my body, and I don't know what it's thinking either. I don't know what it's feeling. I can't work it out. It's doing the things I would do, saying the things I would say, but I know I'm not in it, thinking or feeling or directing . . . and if I'm not there, and it still acts like Thorn, then how can I know there's anything inside Clive that's acting like him? Or inside the others.

Puppets, she thought. *They could all be puppets.*

Her head hurt, or rather the idea of her head hurt.

And then, looking over her body's shoulder, she saw a shadow appear on the frosted glass of the lab door.

A crescent-moon chin and Mr-Punch nose edged into view from one side, a lock of floppy hair bounced across the forehead.

The Scissorman.

She imagined the slow grate of its great big scissor blades sliding one against the other, thought of what the cat had said. Was this really the solution she needed? How she could get back into her body? The Scissorman?

That thing had been so alien, and this day so interesting (if puzzling, worrying, confusing, absurd), in that moment she was sure she didn't want to meet him again. It unnerved her nerveless self.

"All right everyone, back to work, show's over!" said Miss Passell, clapping her hands together. "You OK, Thorn?" she asked.

Thorn turned and the teacher was right there, dome-belly pressed against the desk lip.

"No, Miss," said Thorn.

"Yes, Miss," said Thorn's body.

Thorn turned away, turned back to look at the classroom door and found herself looking at her own front door instead.

Another change.

TWENTY

THE SKY ABOVE her was dark.

There were pinprick twinkling stars, high up.

Her breath would have misted into clouds of dragon fire if she'd had any breath to breathe out.

This was another time, again.

In the blink of a moment, just turning around, she had travelled, slipped, been unstuck.

And then there was a hand reaching out and ringing the doorbell, and there was laughter. It was quiet, awkward laughter, but, still, laughter all the same.

"Don't worry," a voice said.

"Yes, yes," said another voice.

There were two women on the doorstep, waiting for

the door to open. Thorn guessed they were in their early twenties maybe. One had short blond hair, just touching her collar, poking out from under a striped woolly hat. The other was darker, hatless, with a glittering stud in her nose.

There were footsteps inside the house and the door opened and Thorn's mother was stood in the light.

"Thorn," she said. "How lovely. And . . ."

Pause.

"Mum," said the young woman with the nose-ring.

Oh, Gods! That's me, thought Thorn. *That's my body. How old am I now? But I was just in class . . .*

And then she recognised the other young woman. It was an older version of–

"This is Meadowblossom," Thorn's body said.

"Yes," said her mother. "You did say you were bringing your . . . friend . . . with you."

What's going on? thought Thorn.

"Well, come on in. You're letting all the warmth out."

TWENTY-ONE

IT WAS LONGEST Night Festival.

The paper-chain decorations were up and the tree was shedding on the carpet, and there were presents wrapped and stacked underneath it.

They were sat round the dining-room table.

Thorn's mum and dad were sat at either end.

Along one long side sat Thorn's body and Meadow-blossom. On the other side were her brother, Gregor, and a woman called Blade.

Gregor looked so old.

He'd cut his hair down to a faint shadowy fuzz and his chin was covered with dark stubble. He was dressed in a drab green jumper with a pair of crossed guns embroidered on the breast.

(Thorn realised she'd seen him look like this, or more or less like this, before, at the art show – and then a lightbulb flickered in her head and she realised that she'd seen this version of herself before too, in that same gallery, in front of the painting, talking to . . . had that man with her been Clive? She laughed, even as a feeling of doom sank in her – *this isn't going to be a good night.* She didn't remember it, yet, but she just knew, from the atmosphere, from being able to look at people's faces when they didn't know they were being looked at . . . this wasn't a happy family.)

Gregor's girlfriend, Blade, wore a matching jumper to his (drab green, crossed guns) and looked remarkably, perfectly, dully normal. After Thorn looked away she could hardly remember anything about her.

By contrast, Meadowblossom was dressed in bright colours, swirls of rainbow, and Thorn's body wore a top with a slogan on it that said: *Fight fire with art!* There was a small kingfisher tattoo on her upper arm, only uncovered now and then as her sleeve moved.

There was definitely awkwardness in the air.

The food was piled high, as usual for Longest Night, with curlicues of steamy delicious aromas twisting and mixing in the air. Her mum always laid on a good feast.

Thorn's body spooned roast potatoes onto her plate and Thorn watched, fascinated.

This was her future, what she would become.

She had never expected to look cool, had never even thought that someone so old (in her twenties!) could actually *be* cool, but she had to admit, if this was how she was going to turn out, it wasn't too bad.

(Forgetting herself for a second she thought, *Wait till I tell Sam and Katt*, and then remembered. She couldn't tell them. Not yet, not today, and besides, what would they say? What *could* they say?)

"How's the university?" said her mum.

"Oh, it's fine," said Thorn's body. "I'm working on a painting for my final show. It's about hope. How everyone's stuck in this world – this bad world where the demagogues are shouting louder and louder, stoking their hate, spiking their hurt – but how if you care, if you try, you can swim the other way. Fly away. Fly out of the dirt, out of the mess."

There was a vague grunt from across the table, as Gregor piled slices of meat onto his plate.

"That's interesting, dear," said her mum. "Any nice boys in your class?"

"I told you, Mum," Thorn's body said, glancing sideways at Meadowblossom and smiling, "not my cup of tea."

It took Thorn a moment to understand.

Well that's Clive out of the picture, she thought. *Poor old Clive! But Meadowblossom? How had that happened?* (It was one thing to think she fancied you, had a crush, but a whole different matter to find you fancied her back – or your body did, later on . . . if this was actually her future, and not a dream.)

Meadowblossom was from the Nextdoor Country. They were strange people there. A few hours ago she'd've said "Freaks!" like everyone else, but Thorn didn't like that word now. Something was happening to her – had happened to her (maybe the thoughts of her body over there, twenty years old and with a girlfriend, had seeped into her, maybe she'd just seen too much on this strange day). Nevertheless, those people in the Nextdoor Country were not like us, that was true.

Her father said, "Pass me the greens."

TWENTY-TWO

IT WAS LATER.

Meadowblossom had gone to the bathroom.

Gregor leant across the table and was waving his sprout-loaded fork at Thorn's body.

"How could you, sis? She's one of *them*."

"What do you mean?"

"You know what I mean. She's from *over there*."

"And?"

"Well, they're not like us."

Thorn felt uncomfortable. Felt a sense of foreboding. A memory about to be made.

"No," said Blade, backing Gregor up. "Not like us at all. Have you seen how she holds her fork?"

Thorn hadn't noticed anything odd about how Meadow-blossom held her fork.

"You can't trust them. They're always looking for a reason to fight. They want our land. At the border . . . across the Mixing Places . . . they're itching for a reason to start trouble."

"But she's been here for, oh, I don't know, fifteen years? More, I think," Thorn's body protested. "She's one of us."

"Her hair," said her father, while chewing and not looking at her. "It keeps waving, like there's a wind ruffling it. It's not normal. It's a glamour."

"Don't be daft, Dad. That's just how it is. There's nothing she can do about that, is there? And anyway . . ." Thorn's body threw its knife and fork down on its plate with a clatter, ". . . anyway, that's not what I meant to say. *Urgh!* I don't mean to defend her cos she's lived here for so long, or cos she's not one of *them* any more . . . if I do that, I'm just agreeing with you . . ."

Her body was raising its voice now, while trying to keep it down. Thorn really got the feeling it meant what it was saying.

"By arguing like that I'm agreeing with you . . . agreeing

that there's something wrong with people from the Nextdoor Country . . . saying that *she's* an exception. But no! I won't do that. You should accept Meadowblossom because she's a human being, just like us, and that's the end to it."

"Quite right," said Gregor, leaning back with a smug grin. "I mean, if she *was* a human being. But I don't know that those folk in the Nextdoor Country actually *are* human. I mean, not the same stock as us. Science has never proved it, as far as I know."

"You're talking bullshit," Thorn's body snapped.

Thorn saw that there were tears bulging at the corners of her body's eyes. Its cheeks were flushed red. So were its ears.

"Language," said her father, loudly, banging the table with the heel of his hand. Its finger pointed in her direction, even as he didn't look. "I won't have you talking like that to your brother at this table. He's a hero of his country, and what are you? A bloody dossing art student."

If Thorn had had a stomach she would've been sick to it.

Her father never shouted.

He'd never raised his voice to them, not when they were kids, even when they were being annoying.

He'd bury his head in the newspaper and pretend to not hear anything until her mum, his wife, would drag him into whatever the situation was, and he'd huff and say, "Now, now. You're giving your mother a headache. Hush down you two," and that would be the end of it.

But this raised voice at the dinner table . . .

Well, tempers always stretched thin at Longest Night.

Families argued.

That was the way of the world.

"He's my little hero," said her mum, reaching over and patting the back of Gregor's hand.

"Did I miss anything?" said Meadowblossom, coming back into the room.

Thorn wondered how long she had been lingering in the hall before coming in, how much she'd heard.

"Tell us about your work, son," Thorn's dad said, ignoring her.

TWENTY-THREE

GREGOR SAT UP straight and tugged absent-mindedly at his jumper.

"I really can't say too much, because it's classified, you understand."

"Of course."

"But I work out of a classified location, that I can't tell you about, flying classified missions, that I can't tell you about, into enemy territory."

"Computer games," said Thorn's body.

"Drones," said Blade. "Via instantaneous computer link. It's not a game."

"Looks like a game," said Thorn's body, "from what I've seen. Boys sat in dark basements with controllers in their hands and VR goggles on their faces."

"Shush, Thorn," said her father.

"Where do you fly these drones? Where do you send them?" asked Meadowblossom, in a low, calm voice.

"Into enemy territory," said Gregor. "I can't say more than that."

"But we are not at war," said Meadowblossom. "Not at war with anyone. So there is no enemy."

Gregor laughed.

Thorn wished he was still that boy stood on the side of the pool, embarrassed and vulnerable, because this Gregor was stone.

"Oh, that's what you'd have us think, isn't it?" His voice hung with icicles. "But we know what you lot are planning, preparing. Maybe you're not *actually* our enemy, formally, legally, but the day's not far off."

"Me? I?" said Meadowblossom, either confused or pretending to be confused. "My lot?"

"She's one of us," Thorn's body said. "You idiot. You bigoted, arrogant idiot. She's from here!"

"No, no," Meadowblossom said, looking into Thorn's body's eyes, letting her accent grow thicker, stronger. "He's right, isn't he? I'm *not* one of you. I'm a monster from beyond the Mixing Places."

She flashed her teeth.

Didn't hiss.

Left a long moment's silence.

"Maybe we should move on to dessert," said Thorn's mum.

"No," said Gregor, as Blade put her hand on his. "I just want to say, I have nothing to be ashamed of. I'm not a warmonger. I fly purely defensive missions. *We* fly purely defensive missions. We take out enemy positions pre-emptively, before they're ready to hit us. I keep us all safe." He wasn't struggling to keep his voice calm. It was stone. It was moonlight on metal. "We all know they're planning it. We all know they want it. We are just defending ourselves. Keeping people like you, little sister, safe in your beds."

"You kill them before they've done anything!" Thorn's body shouted. "Not in my name!"

"It's murder," said Meadowblossom, softly.

"No civilians are killed."

"It's murder," Meadowblossom repeated.

"They would do worse to us," Gregor said. His face was pale, his mouth unmoving.

Blade was nodding.

"Now look. Look. Look. We don't strike civilian targets," she said. "We're not monsters."

"But it's classified anyway," Thorn's dad said. "You shouldn't be talking about it here. Let's have that dessert, Love."

"We need to leave," Thorn's body said. "I don't feel well, and I've got a big day tomorrow."

"It's a holiday," said her mum. "Stay. We'll talk no more politics, I promise."

TWENTY-FOUR

THORN LEFT THE dining room and its inhabitants to its uneasy silence.

She willed herself out to the back garden.

The space where her heart would've been (should've been) was aching, even without the hormones and other juices.

She floated above the patio, looking up at the far distant stars above the roofs opposite.

She hardly understood any of it.

She was just a fourteen-year-old girl unstuck in time.

Mostly a fourteen-year-old girl. The scene she'd just seen rolled in her like a memory, touching all the sides, colouring her in as if she'd been there herself. It was slowly coming back to her, so maybe she was more than fourteen – older, stranger, wiser! Sadder . . .

She'd never thought about the politics of the world.

(She had, of course, a little. They were messed up, when they weren't boring. She wasn't ignorant, but they talked about sillier, more fun, more interesting things at school. She missed Sam and Katt. She missed just having a laugh. Simple things. Silly things. But she wasn't at school. Maybe she'd left school years and years ago, and was just remembering . . .)

She'd known for years that she and Gregor weren't cut from the same cloth. She was happy to see she'd turned out (would turn out?) how she'd turned out, rather than how he had. (If this was really the future.)

Working for the military was not in her plan.

Thorn had never really thought about being an artist or an art student, either, but had you offered her those two possible roads to go down, then she knew which one she would have preferred to strike out along, even without this glimpse of the future.

She had a sudden memory of a careers advisor at school who had said, "If you join the army, or the navy, or the air force, even as a cook, or a mechanic, or an accountant, you are signing up to kill people. You are joining an organisation whose fundamental job is to kill. Be very sure you know what you're signing up for, and that you're happy to be a part of that."

Mr Beaumont that was, the old deputy head. Basher Beaumont, they'd called him, for no real reason other than the hearty, old-fashioned sound of it. He'd been doubling as a careers advisor in the period immediately after the army recruitment man had taken assembly, with his exciting video all about comradeship and adventure and building wells in less developed parts of the world.

"You might do all that stuff," Mr Beaumont had said, "but still, underneath it all, the price you pay is being someone willing to pull that trigger. I can't stop you, but I still beg of you, don't do it."

He'd been asked to leave the school the next term, she remembered, and although no one said it was because of that speech, she now wondered if it had been. (Who had told on him?)

But, Thorn suddenly thought, *that can't be a memory, cos you don't get careers advice until you're in the year above mine.*

What the hell's going on with me?

As she thought that, there came a crashing like thunder, rumbling in from some far-off distance, closer and closer until it was all around her,
and then, like the end
of all things, the
lights went out.

TWENTY-FIVE

A FLICKER. A buzz.

The lights came back on.

"Exquisite Corpse," said Mr Rockinghorse, the Art teacher.

Thorn was in one of the classrooms again, surrounded by teenagers in their school uniforms.

She looked around for her own body and saw it, in its usual place, over by the back.

"What?" said a kid in the front row.

"Exquisite Corpse," repeated the teacher. "We're going to play a game of Exquisite Corpse this session."

There was a murmur of confused disapproval from the class.

This didn't sound entirely appropriate.

Even Thorn wondered what was going on, but at the same time she had a feeling that Mr Rockinghorse was someone she could trust. (Where did that feeling come from? He was just another teacher. Wasn't he?)

"Hush down," he said. "Let me explain how it works."

Thorn's body was looking out the window, not really paying attention.

It was sat next to a kid Thorn didn't remember. A short girl with glasses.

How did she not remember her? This was her class. This was her Art class right now and she should remember everyone in it. Or not *remember*, exactly, because you don't need to remember the things that are happening right now, every day. She shook her not-head and let the thought go.

She looked around the rest of the class.

Meadowblossom and Honeysweet were sat at a desk by themselves, over by the wall, under the poster of 'Great Art Movements in History'. The kids from the Nextdoor Country.

Thorn hadn't remembered them having to sit by themselves, but now she looked properly, she could see there was a sort of demarcation zone around them. No one wrote rules to say it was so, and no one said you had to stay away, and no one did particularly, not especially, but all the same . . .

Thorn didn't want to finish that thought.

Because she'd never noticed it before, that meant she'd been a part of it, or it had been a part of her. (*Was* a part of it, *was* a part of her.) How odd. How disturbing.

She watched as the two girls' hair swayed slightly in those strange unfelt winds.

"It was a game the super-realists used to play," Mr Rockinghorse said. "Everyone takes one of these bits of paper. Yes, that's it. Pass them back. Then, when you're all settled, up at the top of the sheet you draw a head. Any sort of head, but don't take up too much of the paper, just a bit, a quarter or a fifth, maybe. And make sure you draw the neck going down."

The room filled with scribbling.

Pencils on paper.

"Then fold the paper back, so the head is hidden and only the lines of the neck show. Yes. That's it. That's it. Now take your folded sheet of paper and give it to someone else. No. Not the person next to you. Someone across the room.

That's it. Share them out so everyone gets one. Random. Random."

The room became a train station. People passing here and there, back and forth.

Thorn watched as Meadowblossom and Honeysweet swapped with one another.

"Oh, go and swap with them," she said, willing her body to listen.

It didn't. Instead it swapped with Sam, who sat across the way.

Her body and Sam smiled as they swapped, and sort of rolled their eyes at this silly thing Rockinghorse was making them do.

"No, don't unfold the paper! Wilhelm, swap again. You saw your head. I want it to be fresh, to be free. Swap again."

Wilhelm swapped with Sam, not grumpily, but without grace. Being called out like that had dented his pride.

"Now, without unfolding, continue the neck lines down and draw a body. Any body. Whatever you can imagine."

Thorn watched over her body's shoulder as her body drew a body.

It was dressed in a ballgown's bodice, with tentacular

arms wiggling out, and with tufts of hair in the armpits (tentaclepits?).

Thorn didn't remember drawing that, but she liked it. It was unexpected and funny and absolutely the sort of thing her brother would hate.

"It doesn't make sense," she heard him say.

"Good," she said.

The class then folded the paper again, passed it on, drew legs.

Folded, passed, drew shoes and the ground their figures stood on.

"This is just a kids' game," someone complained. "This is silly."

This is my life, Thorn thought. *This is my long today. Folded over, and random.*

"The artists thought of it," Mr Rockinghorse said, "as a way to access the unconscious. To free their brains from the *this-then-this-then-this*-ness of the quotidian world."

"Use words we can understand," someone shouted.

"The *everyday* world," he said. "By

ignoring what comes before and not worrying about what comes next, they felt free, freer. And then when the piece of paper was unfolded . . . Everyone, unfold the sheet you've got . . . When it was unfolded they discovered these wild and beautiful creatures, characters, that would never have existed had they known what they were doing. If they'd thought about it, these works of art would never have come to be."

"It's rubbish," said a kid near the front.

"This one's got too many . . . who drew this?"

"It's weird."

Thorn watched her body unfold the sheet it had ended up with. The one on which it had drawn the ground: a wavy seaweed-y sandscape with heavy dark boots, metal and cold. Puffs of sand drifting either side of them.

Above them thick black trousers.

Above them a belt on which were attached weights, and a body with tubes coming out of it, snaking off the side of the sheet.

And above them, a smiling face peering out of a big brass old-fashioned diver's helmet.

"That's not really the idea, Thorn," said Mr Rockinghorse

as he passed by her desk. "You were supposed to pass it round. It was supposed to be, sort of, random, you know?"

Thorn's body looked up at him.

"I did, sir," it said. "It went all over the room. I only finished it, this one. I just did the feet and the seaweed."

"Well, either you peeked, or coincidence is smiling on you, big time."

"I didn't peek," her body said.

As Thorn looked at her body's face, she could see it was close to tears.

Art is supposed to move you, she thought.

"Well," said Mr Rockinghorse, kindly, smilingly. "The universe is clearly trying to tell you something. Maybe—"

"Sir!" shouted a voice from the other side of the room. "Sir! Someone's drawn penises on my picture!"

The teacher rolled his eyes at Thorn (not at her body) as he turned away, and Thorn felt for a moment that he'd seen her, but then she realised he'd just been rolling them for himself.

"Boys!" he shouted across the room, with joke-exasperation in his voice. "Gods! It is a truth universally acknowledged that teenage boys have a limited number of interests and motifs, and that sometimes they manifest in art, and that sometimes they're not appropriate for schoolwork. Let's see the offending article."

Thorn could make a good guess at who'd turned an art lesson into a rude doodle class. Almost any of them.

She looked down at her body holding the picture of the deep-sea diver.

"It's not my fault," the diver said. "I wasn't here until just now."

"I know," said Thorn.

"The universe made me. I'm to give you a clue."

"A clue?"

"Yes," said the diver, its voice bubbling and waving as it spoke. "You're feeling lost. Unstuck. But you've got an anchor. It'll be all right in the end."

"I'll go back?" she asked. "I'll go back into my body?"

"Oh yes," said the diver. "That's all you are, really."

"Just a body?"

"At the end of the day, and at the start. So long as your heart's pumping."

The diver tugged on his safety line which snaked off up the top of the page.

"Hey! Hey!" he shouted, tugging again. "Keep pumping up there! You guys, keep pumping!"

"Who are you talking to?"

"Whoever's on the boat," he said. "Whoever's manning the pumps. Sometimes they need reminding, you know?"

"No," she said. "I don't really know."

She felt buoyed up though, by this little conversation, this little moment of being seen. She'd been alone, drifting, observing, for too long, without anyone seeing her. She hoped the cat would come and explain things, they were the only one who really seemed to know what was going on, but this jolly diver . . . well, at least he was on her side too.

"I really don't know," she said again, "but thank you."

"OK! Class!" Mr Rockinghorse called over the classroom hubbub. "Listen up!"

TWENTY-SIX

"AN ARTIST," HE said, now that everyone was back in their seats and quiet. "An artist is like an eyeball. What does an eyeball do?"

"See things," someone said.

"Yes. An eyeball is the part of your body that sees. An artist is the part of society that sees. Or hears. Or smells."

Someone made a fart noise.

"Oh come on," he said, throwing his hands up in the air, over-dramatically. "I'm trying to tell you something important here."

"Will it be on the test?" someone else said.

Mr Rockinghorse shook his head, almost laughing, almost crying.

"No," he said. "Almost certainly not. My friends, I can promise you, I will almost certainly *never* teach you anything they'd put on a test."

"What's the point, then?"

"The point is being alive. Being awake. The point is we *need* art. We need artists to look at the world around us and show it to us anew. Afresh. Sometimes they reflect it as it is, for good or ill. Sometimes they imagine the possibilities, for good or ill, show us what might happen, what they *fear*, what they *dream*. Sometimes they just want to entertain. But art is how a society looks at itself, sees itself, not through reports and results and government enquiries."

The roomful of kids yawned, but Thorn listened.

She smiled.

"Artists might be how society sees itself," the cat said, jumping up onto the desk and not knocking Thorn's body's pencil case out of the way (*I'd just thought of you*, she thought, *and you appeared!* Her not-a-heart pumped in her not-a-chest). "But it doesn't stop there. There is something bigger than society, bigger than countries and nations and cultures."

"What do you mean?"

The cat looked up.

The ceiling had vanished and the night sky spread above them, endless and black and speckled with lights.

"The universe," the cat said. "For billions of years it was empty. Nothing. Not a sausage. And then, in some tiny pond on some bare rock somewhere, something changed. Something became aware. A collection of chemicals and elements, proteins and acids, happened upon a shape that *knew* something. For the first time, something knew where it was. Something knew it was different to the rest of the mud. Some mud sat up and looked around! And the universe began to wake up from its timeless slumber."

"Where was that?" Thorn asked. "Was it on Earth? Here?"

"Maybe," the cat said. "Maybe not."

"How long ago?"

"Longer than you think."

"It was life?"

"It *became* life. And the universe became alive. With each new instance of life – plant or animal or other – the universe woke up a little more."

"When artists are silent," Mr Rockinghorse was saying, "society falls asleep. When artists are silenced, it begins to die. You'll see it again and again through history. Only

totalitarian societies kill their poets. Only dictatorships burn their painters and break the fingers of their pianists. We are sleepwalking, sleepwalking into . . ."

He let his words trail off, as some kids the other side of Thorn's body began muttering secret things.

"Little loops," the cat said. "Little loops of self-reflecting consciousness."

"What?" asked Thorn.

"That is what you are. What I am. We're tiny sensory nodes in time that witness the universe. We are the tastebuds of everything. We are the sense organs of the universe. We feed back to some different level of existence, where the universe thinks its eons-long, slow, deep, slow deep thoughts. Isn't it amazing?"

"I'm a tastebud?" said Thorn. "Doesn't sound that amazing."

"Maybe ask your tastebud how it feels, one day."

"Bored, I expect, with the cooking in the canteen here. Offended, perhaps."

"Ha ha," said the cat, jumping down from the table and vanishing behind Thorn's body's bag.

The class was over, kids were leaving.

"I'm gonna tell my dad," said one boy to another as they shoved for the door. "I reckon he's a troublemaker. And what nonsense, what a bloody waste of time, drawing rubbish like that."

Thorn watched as her body lingered at its desk.

The diver, who was still standing on the seafloor willing those on the boat to keep on pumping, said, to no one in particular, "Too deep. We're all in too deep."

TWENTY-SEVEN

THORN'S BODY STOOD up slowly.

She was the last one left.

It folded the diver up, tucked it between the pages of a book and slipped it into her bag.

Although there was a blank look on her body's face, a look that gave no hint of its insides, Thorn remembered what she felt.

Although the details hadn't arrived, no fast burst of memory filling in the corners of her mind, she just knew she'd been through this day before – that it had been important (would be important).

She was puzzled. Worried.

(Her body was puzzled, worried.)

"Sir," it said, walking up to Mr Rockinghorse's desk.

"Yes?"

"I didn't cheat, sir."

"What?"

"With the picture."

"No. Of course you didn't. I hope it didn't sound like that was what I was saying."

They stood in silence for a moment.

"Is that all, Thorn?" he said, pulling his jacket down from the hook on the wall.

Thorn's body looked at its shoe for a second, then looked up.

"Do they really kill artists?" she asked. "I mean, in bad countries?"

Mr Rockinghorse looked at her, the light from the window behind him turning his curly hair into a halo.

"In bad countries? Oh yes," he said. "Yes, they do."

And he pulled his jacket on, and as he did so he blocked out the light and Thorn, and her body, were plunged into darkness.

TWENTY-EIGHT

THERE WAS AN explosion of sound.

The darkness was studded, punctured, stabbed by flashes of coloured lights, and Thorn's ears were filled with thumping, thundering music.

There were bodies all around her, moving, fighting, wrestling, arguing, shouting so loud they still couldn't be heard under the pulsing, thumping, repetitive beat.

There were so many people there, such a crowd, such a mob, jostling and jumping, that she wondered how it was possible. How could each of those heads on each of those shoulders down there contain a person, contain a whole world – how could there be so many different points of view?

Thorn felt overwhelmed, swallowed by the size of it all.

It was a battleground.

And then she understood.

The scrum around her wasn't the sweaty fight she'd first seen it as, it was a party, a nightclub, a rave.

They were dancing, not fighting.

And she backed away, away and up, above the crowd, up to a safe spot near the ceiling.

It was an ocean of bodies below her, tossing and waving like a stormy sea.

She half expected to see a trawler power in from one side, or an ocean liner come from the other.

Why was she here?

Where was she here?

She knew her body must be down there, somewhere. Down there treading water in that rising and falling mass of people.

It was so loud, so dark, so horribly crowded and sweaty and, again, loud.

Thorn had never been to a club like this, of course (this

was no end-of-year disco but something bigger, hotter, closer), but she'd seen them on the telly often enough.

I'll have to wait, she thought. *I'll just have to wait and find out why I'm here.*

She guessed, maybe, she'd been sent here, shown this, brought to this place, this memory, this future, for a reason, perhaps. Pushed this way, pulled that. It wasn't too different to her normal life. Every day a timetable: be here, look this way, do this! And at home: dinner at this time, bed at that time, homework then, telly now. People who said they made all their own decisions were mostly wrong, she reckoned.

And as she thought the music played on.

TWENTY-NINE

TIME WENT BY.

Foot-stomping track followed foot-stomping track.

And then, without warning, the music shut off. The darkness vanished and was replaced by bright-white warehouse lights, shining down from the ceiling like a hundred sudden suns.

Below her the silence was filled with shouts, cries, screams.

The doors at one end of the large rectangular room burst open with a splintering sound, and figures in black started streaming in, like an infection, like an injection into a healthy body.

"Cops!" someone shouted.

"It's a raid!" someone else shouted.

"Clear out!"

The words were passed around the crowd, even as a voice over a loudspeaker screeched with feedback into the light.

"Everyone stay where you are. Remain calm. This is an authorised search of premises. Remain where you are and cooperate with the officers passing among you."

But at the far end of the room, the large room, at the end where the turntables and speakers were set up, where there was a raised platform above the dancers like a stage, two small fire doors were flung open and the tide began carrying partygoers away, through, out into the dark of the night.

And Thorn felt herself flow with them, following her body, down below, wherever it was.

THIRTY

IN THE CAR park behind the warehouse, a cordon of police cars with flashing lights were providing their own disco ambience to the darkness, and young people were running.

This is the evening it happens, thought Thorn.

Some were intercepted, tackled, by men and women in uniform, bundled to the ground. Others made it past the cars and escaped off into the night.

But the evening what *happens?*

There was a memory there, somewhere, but she couldn't see it. It nudged at her, like a cat at the ankle, but for whatever reason she couldn't look down, to see exactly what it was.

Something was happening.

Would happen.

Had happened.

She watched the scene, still thinking how strange it was that her body must be down there somewhere, going about its business without the faintest inkling she was looking for it.

She'd never imagined she was the sort of person who would go to a huge party like this. She didn't even have a favourite pop group, or an outfit to wear.

And then she caught sight of a tall boy, a man really, who was running with two girls – women, she corrected herself – off into the fields beyond the industrial estate.

And as she drifted down to see them, their faces glowing in the light from mobile phones, she recognised Clive, now grown up with a little goatee beard and a baseball cap. And the two young women, one was her body, looking much as she had at the Longest Night Festival, and the other was . . . Who?

She circled round them, looking closer.

Ah! Yes!

It was Sam, all grown up too.

And then she remembered what had happened, and the night slotted into place.

THIRTY-ONE

THORN WAS AT the local university, studying art.

Mr Rockinghorse had encouraged her to follow her talent, follow her interests, despite her parents' disapproval.

And both Sam and Clive were there too.

She remembered laughing with them both, late at night in student digs, remembering their school days, so long ago.

How odd, Thorn thought, *I'm remembering the future. Remembering things that haven't happened to me yet. I'm a fourteen-year-old girl, but I'm also twenty, and I guess I'm also that eight-year-old by the swimming pool. I'm all these people and they're all the same person, and I can remember being all of them, and they're all me. How odd! How crazy! When am I going to wake up from this? And when I wake up, how old will I be? Which me is the me that's dreaming?*

It spun her head, made her feel like the universe, looking down over everything, in at everything, all at once, while also being a part of it – being many parts of it . . . she couldn't think of words that pinned the feeling down, and besides she was intent on following her body.

It was wearing paint-spattered dungarees, and had flecks of paint on its face, not put there as snazzy make up, but spritzed from a paint brush.

Sam and Clive were both dressed more appropriately for clubbing.

But Thorn's body had been in her uni studio, working on a painting when she'd got a message from Clive reminding her it was the night of Sam's big show. She was dancing, not the lead, but not third-from-the-left-in-the-back-row, in a new ballet that night.

Thorn's body had lost track of time, and raced out, with a paint brush in her pocket and no chance to get changed.

After the show she'd reluctantly agreed to go on afterwards.

Sam was buzzing. She hadn't messed up a single one of her scenes, whereas the girl dancing the lead had stumbled at least once, and so she was feeling on top of the world.

It was only right to celebrate.

And so they'd ended up at the secret club, a little out of town.

And now they were in the farmer's fields, running away from the police, looking towards the lights of the dual carriageway, beyond which was safety.

"Why did we run?" Sam said, not quite out of breath.

"Why wouldn't we?" said Clive, panting. "If we'd stayed we'd've been in trouble. We'd've been put on a list or something."

"It was just a party," Sam said.

"Well, maybe you should've stayed," Clive said. He didn't snap, but there was a blur in his voice, like he'd been drinking. "Got yourself a nice set of metal bracelets and a photo in the files."

Of course they've been drinking, Thorn thought, feeling prudishly young for a moment. *They're old enough and they're out at a nightclub.*

"Running?" Sam said. "I didn't have a choice. You pulled

us and then we were out and we were running before I knew what was happening. I couldn't stop then, or they'd've wanted to know why I was running . . ."

"Did you see if Kev got away?"

"I don't know. No."

All this time, Thorn's body hadn't been joining in.

Then, suddenly, as they slowed almost to a stop, it staggered and slumped.

It fell in the furrows of the field, twisted, and then climbed to its feet, facing the wrong way.

"Ow," it said, and held its hand up to its head.

"You OK?" said Sam, suddenly sober. The combination of

the cold night air and the escape from the cops had washed the last of the alcohol from her system.

"She took a hit," Clive said, looking back towards the warehouses, where they could still see the coloured lights on the police cars spinning silently. "As we went past the cars. One of them clipped her with a baton. But she kept running, I thought she was OK."

"There's blood," said Sam, holding Thorn's body's hand. "Look, she's bleeding. Bloody hell."

"I'm OK," said Thorn's body, trying to stand up straight. "I'm . . . Hang on . . ."

THIRTY-TWO

AT THE HOSPITAL they told the receptionist that she'd fallen. Banged her head on the ground.

They didn't mention the police baton. Or the raid. Or where they'd been.

"She'd had a shandy or two," they said, with a laughing roll of the eyes. "In the Union."

Everyone knew students liked a drink. It was all the explanation they needed.

The receptionist had them wait on hard plastic chairs in the whitest of light, among the other drunks and unfortunates who'd ended up in Casualty that evening.

"You're good friends," Thorn's body said, blurrily.

And then she was called forward to be seen by the doctor.

Thorn followed her body into the little curtained cubicle.

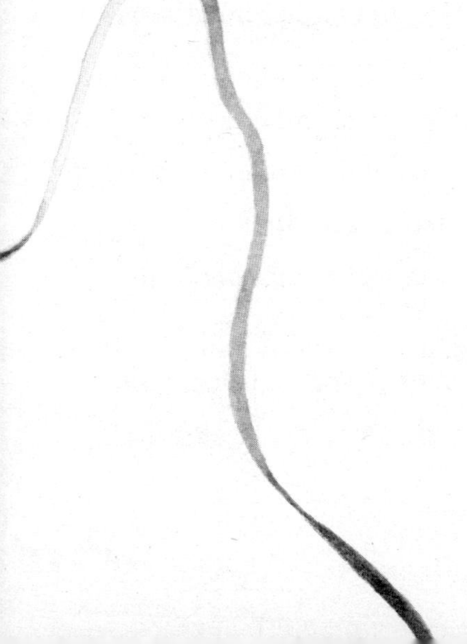

THIRTY-THREE

AND THERE WAS Meadowblossom.

This was *that* night.

She hadn't remembered until she remembered.

Meadowblossom hadn't gone to university.

It wasn't that people like her weren't *allowed*, but some things were just understood.

Instead she had become a trainee nurse, and was working on the nightshift at the General Hospital, stitching up the drunks and removing the saucepans kids had got their heads stuck in. (Or whatever story happened to walk in that particular night.)

She stood to the side as the doctor shone their light into Thorn's body's eyes and said, "Concussion. Minor abrasion.

Doesn't need stitches. Don't drink for the next few days. Get plenty of rest. Make sure someone checks up on you. Don't drive. Don't play rugby. And don't fall over again. You'll be fine. Nurse? Clean the wound. Give her the usual leaflet. And then she can go home. OK?"

And then the doctor was gone and it was just Meadowblossom and Thorn's body.

There was silence for a minute as Meadowblossom clipped away the hair from immediately around the cut.

"Do you remember me?" she asked.

"Sorry?" said Thorn's body.

"We were at school together. It's a few years ago now."

"Of course," said Thorn's body, looking up at her. "You're Meadowblossom."

Her hair was hidden beneath a cap.

"Yes," said Meadowblossom. "And you're Thorn. You punched me once."

And that was how it began.

With antiseptic-soaked cotton wool being dabbed on a fresh cut.

"Ow," said Thorn's body, flinching. "That stings."

THIRTY-FOUR

ONLY A FEW hours ago Thorn had woken up.

As she floated there, she marvelled at it, still couldn't understand it.

There was a story she remembered hearing once: it was about a man who dreamt he was a butterfly, but then he wondered if actually he was a butterfly dreaming it was a man (dreaming he was a butterfly), and she wondered if maybe he hadn't been a man dreaming he was a butterfly dreaming it was a man dreaming he was a butterfly.

There was no end, no knowing when to stop, when you started thinking like that.

Was she a teenage girl dreaming about her future (which may or may not turn out how she dreamt it), or was she a grown woman dreaming her past, or was she that little girl by the swimming pool, making up stories for all the years ahead?

Round and round and round it goes, where it stops no one knows.

She remembered a thought she'd had earlier in the day, of lying on an operating table, hallucinating all this under the gas, and she wondered *Why these moments? Why this life? (Is there a purpose, am I meant to wake up tomorrow and have learnt a lesson?)* And then she thought that maybe she wasn't under the gas after all, that she only thought that because she was in the hospital right now – maybe she was fine, just asleep somewhere after too much cheese. And if she *was* hallucinating, or dreaming, maybe she wasn't even Thorn . . . Gods!

Round and round and round it goes, where it stops no one knows.

She had the faintest memory of a holiday she'd gone on once (if she could trust a memory she wasn't seeing), of being at the seaside. She and Gregor were small, just kids, and their mum and dad had dumped them in an amusement arcade while they went for coffee or a cigarette, or both.

She could almost hear the buzz and rattle and *ding ding*

ding of the machines, and almost saw the solid silver ball roll down the slope of the pinball, bouncing off the flashing protrusions and barriers and mushrooms and rubber bands as it sparkled down to the flippers.

Her fingers jabbed and banged and sent the ball hurtling back up the board, setting off more alarms and fireworks, sent hither and thither, totally not of its own accord – like a butterfly in a storm, at the mercy of the breeze, until . . . until it finally gave up, got forgotten, got missed, and rolled down into the gap between the flippers.

She had the faint memory of sadness as the ball vanished, as her little fingers mistimed the bang and flick, as the butterfly exhausted on its migration stopped flapping and was plucked from the air by the ocean wave.

Oh!

Maybe she was a butterfly, or a pinball, or a patient, or a cat, or a kingfisher . . .

She glanced down at the two young women finishing their conversation below and she saw the kingfisher tattoo, hiding under the sleeve of her body, up at the top of her arm. She wanted to ask her body about it, ask, "Why that bird? Why that tattoo?"

They were laughing, Thorn's body touching its head as it did, wincing with the headache it must've been feeling.

Thorn left the cubicle, pushed herself out into the corridor.

Her body had someone, someone who was noticing her.

She wanted that cat to come back, or that diver, or someone.

She felt so alone, suddenly lost, suddenly down after the high of remembering/seeing this first/not-first meeting.

Above her the fluorescent strip-light was flickering with hisses and pops and buzzes.

"You're not alone," it said. "You've never been alone."

"Oh," she said. "I didn't realise you were listening in."

"Someone's always listening in," the light said with a crackle.

"Always?"

"Well, that's the universe for you. It's grown up now. It's observing itself all the time. Thinking about itself. Oh, sure, there may be corners the light's not reached yet, but most of it's observed, one way or another, I reckon."

"The cat said something about that. I didn't really understand."

"The universe is nothing if it's not being looked at,

listened to, smelt, felt. Sensed. Observed. That's the point of loops like you."

"Not you?"

"Not really me, no. I'm mostly just a figment of your imagination. I'm not alive like you. But you living things, you look at the universe and make it real. It's beautiful, really. I wish I was alive. I wish I was a part of it, like you."

"The cat called me a tastebud."

"That's the sort of thing a cat would say. They think with their mouths, with their tongues."

"What would you say?"

"I'd say the universe is a weave of life absorbing light waves. Light is what travels, what connects this part of the great cosmos to that part. Future to past. Sound doesn't travel through space, only light. You and your sort are more like rods and cones than tastebuds. You absorb the light and make sense of it."

"I don't really understand," Thorn said. "I'm only fourteen. I think."

"You're only fourteen? I'm only a lightbulb! But I'm also the sand that I was before it was made into glass, and a fleck of the star that exploded to make the elements that made the sand, and the energy of the ocean that pounded those beach stones to powder, and I'm the shards of glass and the puff of noble gas vanishing in the wind that will appear when this hospital's knocked down in the war, and I'm whatever happens after that."

"And I'm all ages, is that what you're saying? I'm the elements and atoms that make up my body, and the worms that will eat me afterwards?"

"No," said the lightbulb. "And yes. You can think of the elements and the atoms if you want, but you're different to me. That's your body. Yes, that's you, but more importantly you're a mind. The thing that arises from a body. You're a closed loop."

"What does that mean?"

"It means," the lightbulb began, but Thorn's body emerged from the curtained cubicle, pushed in a wheelchair by Meadowblossom, out to the reception where her friends were waiting, and Thorn found herself following them.

"I'm sorry," she called to the flickering, humming lightbulb. "I've got to go. Another time."

"There's only this time," the bulb said as it failed and went out, leaving those few metres of corridor in shadow. "For you, there's only ever this time."

THIRTY-FIVE

AS THORN FOLLOWED her body through swinging double doors in the hospital corridor, watching it hand Meadowblossom a slip of paper with her phone number on it, she lost them.

One second the doors were swinging shut, crashing noisily, and the next she was in the front room of a perfectly normal house, with brown wallpaper and heavy curtains.

There was a big, old-fashioned telly on the stand in the corner, and a brown leather sofa that seemed familiar.

The door in front of her opened and a woman walked in.

It was her! Her body.

She was older again, maybe getting close to thirty now. She looked tired and was obviously pregnant.

And then she realised, with a start, that it *wasn't* her body, it was her mother.

She looked so young. Had her hair cut short, was dressed in the sort of slouchy clothes Thorn imagined her twenty-something self would wear. Comfy things without much style.

And then her mother turned, responding to a shout from upstairs. A child's voice calling down, needing something.

And the door shut behind her and Thorn was alone.

This was the front room of the house she grew up in. It took her a moment to recognise its shape, its size.

Furniture would move around over the years and that wallpaper would go, but, yes, this was home.

It was the house she lived in now, she realised, even though it felt like a place she was digging into her memories to recognise. Only this morning she'd slouched down those stairs and had breakfast in that kitchen just through there.

Amazing.

And then the door opened a second time.

And her mother walked in again.

She had changed her clothes.

She was carrying a bundle in her arms, wrapped, swaddled, in a white woollen blanket.

This was her body. Come home from the hospital, the first time.

She started crying – no, Thorn's body started crying. Tiny, loud.

Her dad came in behind, carrying bags, looking even more exhausted than his wife.

And Gregor followed in behind him. Small, fluffy, smiling.

"Why's the baby sad?" he said.

Such a little question.

"She's not sad," her mum said, carefully sitting down on the sofa. "She's hungry."

And there was a light in her mum's eyes as she said that, which cut through the tiredness, shone over the grey rings, and it was a light of love. Pure, untarnished love.

And she began to nurse Thorn's body.

And Thorn, floating there, watching the scene that she didn't remember, listened to her body greedily suck milk from her mother's breast.

That's how I grew, she thought. *This is where I come from. And now she makes me toast in the morning instead, and roast dinners, and soup.*

She thought of the carrot soup her mum made whenever one of the kids was ill. It was the only time you ate on the sofa, with the special extra-soft blanket that came out when you were under the weather.

Although, she realised, that *wasn't* the only time you ate on the sofa, although she'd never known. Her first meal in the house had been there, was happening there right now.

Right now, even though she was only passing through this memory or dream or glimpse into the past. Thorn's body seemed so happy as it fell asleep, even as it nuzzled and guzzled her mum's rich milk.

And she saw how Gregor looked.

"Can I hold the baby?" he said, in awe.

"She's asleep," his mum said. "I think she's fallen asleep."

"I'll be quiet," Gregor said. "I'll be kind."

He sat beside his mum on the sofa, and took the little breathing body in his arms and held her so carefully, as if she were a bomb, but with such devotion in his eyes.

"I love her," he said.
Little kids are so certain.
He was humming a tune.
They believe nothing will ever change.

This old man's called Michael Finnegan . . .

They believe what they say.

He grew whiskers on his chinnegan . . .

They don't mean to lie.

The wind blew up and pushed them in again . . .

Whatever happened to him? Thorn thought.

Poor old Michael Finnegan, begin again.

There was a sound like crashing waves, thunder, a rock-slide, and darkness engulfed everything: house, family, Thorn.

THIRTY-SIX

THE NOISE STOPPED, dust settled, the light rose.

"He grew up," said the cat, as if nothing had happened.

Thorn looked down, and the cat, the same cat as always, was lying curled in a patch of pallid sunlight.

She looked up.

The room had changed again.

She was in an attic now. She could tell from the shape of the ceiling, and the window in the little triangular end wall.

Grey daylight dribbled in.

"Where am I now?" she said.

"Look," said the cat, before it turned and walked behind her, vanishing again.

And as she looked round she saw that the sloping

walls were stacked with unframed paintings, leaning against them on the floor.

There were maybe a dozen of them, and on the other side of the room, over by the stairs, was an easel. And on it was an unfinished painting.

On the ground beside it were some brushes and a spilt pot of something. Water, probably, judging by the grey damp stain on the floorboards.

The paintings she could see against the wall looked like abstract blocks of colour, muted reds and greens and browns, which slowly transmogrified as she looked deeper, into landscapes and buildings. They were just a little sideways, a little off-kilter, as if they weren't quite real, or were supposed to look not quite real.

She thought of the Mixing Places, where her country abutted the Nextdoor Country, and of her brother's drone flying above the confusion below into sweeter air and golden sunlight.

And then she saw that across the semi-abstract landscapes figures floated, gauzy strange ghost-like figures, or rings of dancing shapes, hand-in-hand. There were animal-headed people looking on and fearful prey lurking in the hidden corners. And cats! Behind every bush there lurked a cat about to jump out and give you a lecture on something weird.

Tall, frail, mechanical structures populated some of the images too. Something like people or pylons or clocks or watermills, reduced to black lines, wires or girders, wheels and struts. They were dream-machines of unknowable purpose, perhaps even to the artist.

They were strange paintings that Thorn didn't understand, but which she recognised as coming from her own dreams, her own mind, her own decisions, somewhere in the future when she was grown up and had left university and was making her way in the world. She remembered these times, remembered painting in this room as the light changed through the day, while she waited for Meadowblossom to come home from her last shift at the hospital.

She was losing the her who woke up this morning and watched their body haul itself out of bed. In this room, at this moment, she felt sure that *this* was her, this grown up, this artist! How could she have ever thought anything else?

And yet . . . and yet, even as she thought that, she felt like a kid – she was down at the swimming pool, out of her depth, treading water to keep from going under, trying to reach the ladder . . .

Oh! Meadowblossom!

It was with that thought that she looked at the painting on the easel, the unfinished one.

It was different from the others.

It was a portrait, a picture *of* a person, not a picture in which people appeared.

And it was of her.

Of course it was.

Even in paintings their hair seemed to move.

She was good. (Or she would be good, in the future, however far from now (from this morning) this attic was.) She'd captured the look of the Meadowblossom she'd seen in the hospital, the grown-up one that had dabbed her wound in Casualty.

The eyes followed you round the room.

No wonder I fell for her, Thorn thought. *Will fall for her . . . If this is how I saw her . . . will see her . . .*

And then she remembered something else from her future.

Sam.

An argument with Sam in the uni bar one night.

"She's bewitched you . . . enchanted you . . . You know what they're like, Thorn. You can't trust them. It's all a glamour."

And that had been the end of that friendship, after years.

It had hurt, she remembered that. *It will hurt*, she corrected herself. *Might hurt. It's still in my future. Maybe I'll be able to talk sense into her this time . . . next time.*

And then she found herself sinking down.

Down through the floorboards, past pipes and cables and mouse droppings, and down through the bedroom below and further down, down, down.

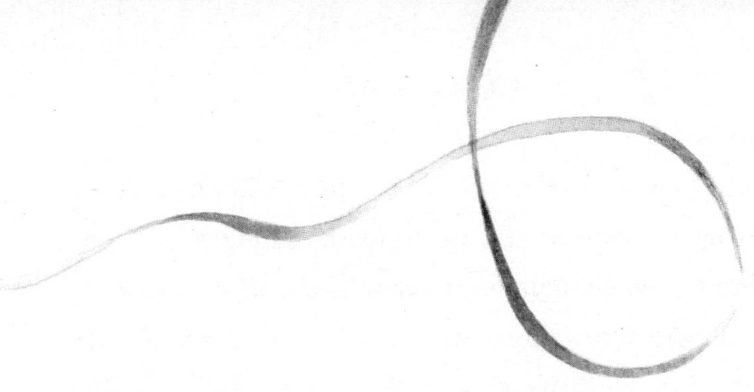

THIRTY-SEVEN

THE WEEPING WOMAN was stroking the cat's fur, twining her fingers through it.

That's my body, Thorn thought. *But it looks like my mum, when she brought me home – as a baby.*

Gods, I don't know which way I'm going! I don't know which way I'm supposed to be looking!

The doorbell rang.

The door knocked.

The woman stood up.

And, oh! . . . My body . . . it's pregnant!

This was a lot.

Thorn didn't know what to do with it.

She'd never expected this.

A part of her wanted to go back to her Maths class and stare at Clive again – things were so simple back then, a few hours and so many years ago! But another part of her wanted to be here – making beautiful strange art in an attic, with her girlfriend downstairs, in a place of her own, never mind the weather outside.

Rain spattered against a window somewhere.

Wind rattled a loose tile way above her head.

The cat looked up at Thorn as her body went to answer the door.

"I came to live here a few weeks ago," it said, off-handedly. "You two were kind enough to open a tin of tuna one night. A cat doesn't say no to an invitation like that. I decided to stay for a while. I think you need me."

"What do you mean?" asked Thorn.

"Just wait," said the cat.

Thorn's body, in its late twenties – still with the nose ring, belly pushing at paint-dotted dungarees – came back into the room, followed by an older man.

He looked around for somewhere to put the umbrella he was rolling, and after a moment dropped it on the floor by the door.

He had a little moustache and looked slightly familiar.

No, more than slightly. He looked very familiar. She'd seen him only a few hours before.

"They took her," Thorn's body said, slumping onto the sofa, hands folded across her belly under the flap of her dungarees. "They practically broke the door down and took her."

The man pulled a chair over from under a small fold-out dining table and sat in it, facing her body.

"Tell me," he said.

And the moment Thorn heard his voice she knew she was right.

Mr Rockinghorse.

"It's the war," her body said. "It was the police. They came an hour after the announcement. They had black gloves and black boots and a list, and their eyes were so happy. Filled with such life, Kurt – joy! – I couldn't stand it."

He reached a hand out. Let it rest in the air between them.

"She's an 'enemy alien'," Thorn's body said. "She's been interned. They took her away. One bag. That was all she could take. One bag, and two minutes to pack it. And as she did they rifled through the shelves, looked at our things.

Touched it all. And there was nothing I could do. I couldn't fight them. And I don't know where she is. They wouldn't say. Couldn't say."

"Oh gods," said Mr Rockinghorse. Kurt.

"What's happening?" asked Thorn. "What's she talking about?"

"They took the other one, Meadowblossom, away," the cat said.

The heart she didn't have stopped beating. The breath she didn't have failed to come. She looked from the cat to her body to Mr Rockinghorse.

You heard about this happening in bad countries, people being disappeared, but not when they had a baby on the way, not when they were good people.

"Why?" she said. "I mean, why? How?"

"The police," the cat purred. "Because you can't have people from over there running around free over here. It's common sense. She'll send messages or coordinates or the like. There is a war on, you know."

"You don't believe that," Thorn said.

"What? That there's a war? There's always a war."

"No, that she'd spy for the Nextdoor Country."

"Of course not, but what does it matter? People don't think like that. They are scared, and they like to scare in return."

Thorn thought of Gregor, of Blade, of her father.

They seemed angry. A quiet, bubbling anger that the wrong word could flare, and she saw that it was fear that fed it. They were small people, she thought, afraid of being trodden on, afraid of being replaced. Maybe they were afraid of something she couldn't imagine.

And then she thought, *How odd!* Meaning, *Earlier today I couldn't tell if all these bodies moving around were people or not, if they were just machines made of meat rolling along the tracks of physical laws, and now I'm* so *sure, so certain they're filled with feelings! There* are *ghosts in these machines!*

"Humans should be more like cats," the cat said, yawning. "They should sleep eighteen hours a day and wash with their tongues. Maybe then they wouldn't want to hurt each other all the time."

"They gave me this." Thorn's body held out a slip of paper. Thorn could see it was a printed form, with black ink scribbles in the underlined spaces. "It's a receipt. They gave me a receipt, Kurt, like she was a piece of meat. An object I can take back to the shop. *One wife, slightly used.*"

Wife!

There was nothing her art teacher, her old art teacher, could say.

He went through to the kitchen and Thorn heard the noise of water running, a kettle being switched on.

The silence in the room with Thorn's body was awkward. The cat had pretended to go to sleep. Thorn's body was absently kneading its fur.

Thorn moved herself towards the kitchen, and then stopped.

There on the wall, by the kitchen door, was a framed piece of paper.

"She's kept them pumping the air for me," the diver said. "All these years. Those guys up on the boat, she kept them pumping."

It was that drawing, the folded and unfolded drawing from all those years ago – from just an hour or two ago – saved and laid flat and framed behind glass. Hung up on the wall.

"She kept you," Thorn said.

"Oh, yes," the diver said. "She took me home and pinned me up. You can see the little hole at the top up there."

"Why?"

"Why not?"

Thorn thought, *That's as good an answer as any, I suppose.*

"What can I do?" said Thorn's body from the sofa.

"Live, I guess," said Mr Rockinghorse, stepping into the kitchen doorway, so close Thorn could see the dust in the wrinkles round his eyes. (She took a floating step back.) "Make sure you don't give up. Don't give up on her. And don't let what they've done stop you working."

"Art?"

He shrugged.

"What good is it?" her body said. "How will it help her? . . . Maybe if I hadn't painted those pictures, maybe they wouldn't have taken her . . . She assumed . . . *we* assumed she was safe. She's in a reserved occupation. And she's been here so long."

Mr Rockinghorse shrugged again, shaking his head.

"I remember this," he said, pointing at the picture of the diver, changing the subject. "I remember the day you drew it . . . you and whoever else it was . . . I thought it was a joke, I thought you were playing a joke, until I saw how scared you were . . . genuinely scared. I didn't know what to do then, to make you feel better, and I don't know now."

He stroked the frame with a fingertip, just the softest of brushes.

"Why did you keep it?"

Thorn's body stood up. Stepped closer.

"It reminds me that without air the little diver dies. That without air we all die." The body tapped the glass with a fingernail. "Meadowblossom . . ." It choked. Began again. "Meadowblossom and I, me and her . . . we have been pumping air for years. Pumping air for each other. We've kept each other going. She's let me breathe, given me the space and time and light to work, to be, and . . . oh! I don't know what she gets from me."

"You can sink," said the diver. "You can be lost from sight, look like you've stopped treading water, but if someone's manning the pumps . . ."

"She had someone manning the pumps," said Thorn.

"What do I do now?" Thorn's body repeated, turning away from the diver and facing Kurt.

"I don't know," he said. "I don't know what the answer is. I don't have a good answer. Is it to pick up a gun and fight back? Become like them? Join the protests, the resistance, get yourself locked up as well? Maybe. Maybe.

"Or maybe we make the art we can make, to remember, to record, to keep a record, to be true to ourselves. It's how we communicate, how we share ourselves, our inner selves, with the world. How we prove we're alive, not just bloody robots. And maybe it's important we leave something behind, a record of ourselves for those who come after us to find? Art isn't just how a society talks to itself, but how it hears its past. It's how it talks to the future – it's how we show the future that we understood something, that we had dreams, that we had hope." He shook his head. "I don't know," he said, his shoulders falling, the dust settling. "A paintbrush can't stop a bullet. A book won't deflect a fist."

Thorn's body pushed past him and went into the kitchen.

Thorn followed and found her searching the cupboards for mugs, setting them down on the counter.

"I'm sorry," said Mr Rockinghorse, turning to face her body.

"What if they kill her?" Thorn's body said, reaching out and taking his hand. "What if she never comes back because they kill her in prison? Or she gets a disease? Or there's an accident? Or an 'accident'?"

Thorn wanted to hug her body, to take its hand, to hold it.

"I don't know," said Mr Rockinghorse, tears filling his eyes but not yet falling. "I just don't know. You live and you live, you get older and older, and the answers don't appear. They never give you a manual for living with defeat. But you do it all the same."

"Gods, that's bleak," Thorn's body said, a broken smile flashing for a moment.

"What can I say? I'm a pessimist. I've become a pessimist."

"I thought people were better than that, than this." Thorn's body gestured at the world outside the house.

"Prove it then," said Mr Rockinghorse.

Thorn thought, *He's still a teacher.*

She turned that, 'Prove it,' over in her head like a pebble. Did he mean, 'Give me an example,' or did he mean, 'Be an example'?

"Sometimes I think about it," her body said. "About dying. They say when you die your whole life flashes before your eyes . . . I sometimes think about it, Kurt, and it makes me scared. I've done so many things I don't want to relive."

"Just remember the good bits."

"Yes," said Thorn's body, sniffing a small laugh. "If only. But I'm so scared for her. They hate her so. Just because of what she is . . . She's not safe there . . . Not safe . . . I don't believe I'm ever going to see her again. I keep thinking she's already dead, and I hate myself for it."

"It doesn't matter," said the cat.

"What doesn't?" asked Thorn.

"If she dies."

"How can you say that? It's a wicked thing to say!"

"I just mean," the cat said, "that there's no such thing as death. We are immortal beings. If she dies . . . it's sad for everyone else, of course, but not for her, she's already living for ever."

"Heaven?" Thorn said.

"No." The cat laughed. "Not heaven. Think of it as reincarnation."

"Born again?"

"Yes."

"Another baby, or, like, an animal or something?"

"Oh no. Better than that. The same baby. Always the same baby. You, me, she . . . we're loops, Thorn, loops of self-consciousness. Going round and round. Always and endless."

"I don't get it."

The cat grinned.

"You need to take a step back, to a place you or I can't go. Outside the universe, outside time. Everything exists all at once. Things only seem to happen One then Two then Three, because that's how you move through the universe. But it's all there, all at once. You are a little loop of senses that extends from Place A to Place B, through Time A until Time B. And that can never be destroyed. You will always be that."

"I have absolutely no idea what you're talking about," Thorn said. "I'm a fourteen-year-old girl and we've not studied this at school yet."

"Think of a book. You're a book that's already written. I'm a book that's already written. But as you read it, word by word, you know what came before, but what comes next is a mystery, a surprise. But you could choose to open the book, if you had thumbs, at any page. You could skip ahead, skip back. Maybe a life's like that, looked at from outside."

Thorn's body dropped a mug on the hard tiles of the kitchen floor.

It shattered.

"I'm broken!" Thorn's body shouted. "I'm lost!"

"I'm so sorry," said Mr Rockinghorse, stepping forwards and hugging it. "I'm so sorry."

There was silence for a long moment, broken only by the cat washing itself.

Thorn's body sniffed.

"And I'm sorry, too," it said. "I heard about your job."

"It was always inevitable," Mr Rockinghorse said. "They only kept me on so long because I'm a harmless old duffer, really. But I finally said something or did something, or someone said something, and . . . you know what it is."

Thorn looked away from the two bodies and looked at the white wall above the fireplace. It was blank as a winter sky, but then, as she watched, a spiral of black birds circled across it, *cawing* and *cawing*, and flew into the distance, disappearing and disappearing, until – nothing.

Yes, she thought, *that sums it up.*

But then she saw, perched on the arm of the sofa, just out of reach of the stretching cat, as if it were a branch above the river, the jewel-bright kingfisher.

"What is it with that bird?" she said.

"I think of the kingfisher," said her body, stepping back from the ex-Art teacher's hug, and wiping tears from its cheeks.

"Your bird," he said.

"They live in shit," she said. "Their burrows are full of shit. Never get cleaned out. It's filth and dirt all the way down. But look at them. They fly free of it all. They fly free of the shit."

She laughed, then stopped.

"Would that we had wings too," he said.

Oh, thought Thorn. *I hope she gets free. I hope she and Meadowblossom find somewhere else, where they can be free.* And then she thought, *I guess I mean: I hope* I *get free.*

This was the longest, strangest dream.

"Thank you for coming over," Thorn's body said. "I can't tell you what it means to have someone to listen."

"I know," Mr Rockinghorse said.

"I listen," said the cat.

"What happens next?" asked Thorn.

"She goes home to stay with your mother, while the baby's due."

"Does Meadowblossom come back?"

The cat looked at her, its odd-coloured eyes blinking slowly.

"I can't say," it said. "If she does, my loop ends before it happens."

THIRTY-EIGHT

THERE WAS SILENCE for a time.

Then the noise of rain against a window.

Tea being drunk.

And then the sound of pointed footsteps in the attic, tip-toe-clicking on the floorboards.

Thorn had the sudden image of razor-sharp scissor blades grinding against one another.

There was a crash and a flicker of electric light and the warm smell of the classroom.

Mr Pascal was at the board, tickling it with his pen.

"Ooh, cheeky!"

Thorn's body was gazing out of the corner of its eye at

Clive, who was looking out the window, at the day that was going on beyond the school fence.

Across the classroom, through the forest of other nameable but unimportant pupils, was Meadowblossom, sitting at her desk at the front with Honeysweet. They had their heads together and were pointing at something in the textbook.

I wonder what happened to her? Thorn thought, meaning Honeysweet, but also meaning Meadowblossom. Her memories of the future didn't seem to have the other girl in. Or Katt. What had happened to her?

They just looked like kids, sat there in the Maths room.

Just like kids.

Thorn's non-existent heart ached with all that it knew.

No one in that room knew what was coming.

Thorn turned away.

She had travelled her whole life in just a few hours, seen so many parts of it.

They say it flashes before you.

She had so much going on in her mind.

They say it flashes before your eyes.

She was an eye for the universe to observe itself.

She drifted to the back of the room, observing herself (her body) observing Clive (his body) observing the world beyond the school fence.

What did he see out there?

She drifted down, as low as she could, to just behind his shoulder, to just behind his head, to pass through his head and see the exact view from his eyes.

There was a rainbow, faint and fading above the houses over the road. The sun was shining off their wet roofs, and white clouds were making their escape, high up. Three crows, or maybe they were just pigeons, were sat on the roof ridge, jostling one another, arguing or flirting, in black silhouette.

A van passed by. On its side a logo said *All Shall be Well.*

The traffic lights changed and a mother with a pushchair crossed.

A second van passed the other way: *But Not All the Time.*

"You're telling me," Thorn said, drifting up and away.

She thought of what she'd just seen, her body in tears, heart-breaking, heartbroken, and she thought, not everything can be that hard, surely? It's only moments.

This day has only been moments. Something, some times, must balance with the hurt, otherwise how did she manage? (By 'she' Thorn meant herself; her older self, her younger self, all her selves, and, perhaps, everyone else too.) There must be light out there, outside the burrow. You just had to choose it, to find it, to choose to look for it, to make it, to share it . . . perhaps. Maybe.

Try not to hurt.

She had a feeling, she couldn't say where it came from, but a feeling somewhere inside her non-physical self, that she was nearing the end of this day.

Flashes before your eyes.

She felt thin, felt tired now. She'd seen enough, was ready to sleep.

She was unstuck, but the glue was coming.

"I'm ready to go home," she said, to the world or to the universe. "I've seen enough. I want to sleep and wake up and just be a schoolgirl again. Let me just live my life, please. I don't want to be a viewer any more. Let me watch telly, not me."

The universe said nothing for a moment, in the same way you would say nothing to a tastebud in your mouth that momentarily misfired, sending a darting sour spike up the cranial nerves to your brain, where you probably think the you of you is.

And then.

Your whole life flashes before your eyes.

And then.

There was a staccato, arrhythmic *knock-knock-knock* at the classroom door.

Thorn turned.

There, silhouetted on the glass, seen through the mathematical posters Mr Pascal had tacked up, was the shadow of an oversized pair of scissors.

Snap!

Snip!

Snap!

And the handle turned, and the door slowly opened.

And none of the people who were actually there turned to look.

And through the door stepped the Mr Punch-headed figure of the Scissorman.

THIRTY-NINE

INSTINCT TOLD THORN to run.

Or to drift, at speed.

(This thing was abnormal, was freakish.)

But she seemed to lack the power to move.

(She'd asked for this.)

The grinning face approached her, always, bizarrely, side-on, so the man-in-the-moon shape was visible, with one startling blue eye pinning her down.

(She'd asked the universe.)

The thing tucked its giant scissors into its belt.

Lifted one long pointed leg. Placed it down.

Lifted the other. Placed it down.

Stepped in place like a trained horse, never quite seeming to come closer, while still coming closer.

The perspective was wrong. All perspective was wrong.

Space didn't seem to be working right.

The tables where her fellow students (and her body) sat seemed to shift out the way, to flow like toffee around her and this unlikely being.

"Unstuck," it said. "Gone a bit drifty, have we?"

Its voice scratched and crackled like an ancient record.

Thorn was frightened, never mind not having the right chemicals coursing through her, never mind the belief that this was the cat's solution to her being lost.

She couldn't move.

It pulled from its pocket a large needle, all of three feet long.

The point was so fine it misted into a blue shadow. The eye at the other end was looped through with fine red ribbon that trailed and vanished behind the not-a-man-thing's back.

"All rightio," it said. (*Scratch. Crackle.*) "We'll get you fixed back in place in but a jiffy. Nowt to worry about, my lovely."

"I'm not worried," she said. "I wasn't worried."

She wanted to shout out, to call for Meadowblossom to come and rescue her, but she knew nothing would happen.

But oh! They knew about things like this in the Nextdoor Country, didn't they?

Oh! They enchanted you with their glamour, made you see things.

Yes! That was part of the problem, why getting through the Mixing Places was such a difficult job, because they weren't wholly of this world.

That's what they said.

"Sub-human," Gregor said. "Unhuman. Freaks."

Thorn could see Meadowblossom on the other side of the room, just out of the corner of her eye, and the girl, the teenage girl with the gently blowing blond hair, was looking at her. Not at Thorn's body, at her.

"One little stitch to get you settled."

And she felt a prick, a stabbing sensation, and saw the red ribbon vanishing as it wove into the space she didn't occupy. In and out, in and out.

And Meadowblossom smiled, and Thorn imagined her saying, "I'll see you later."

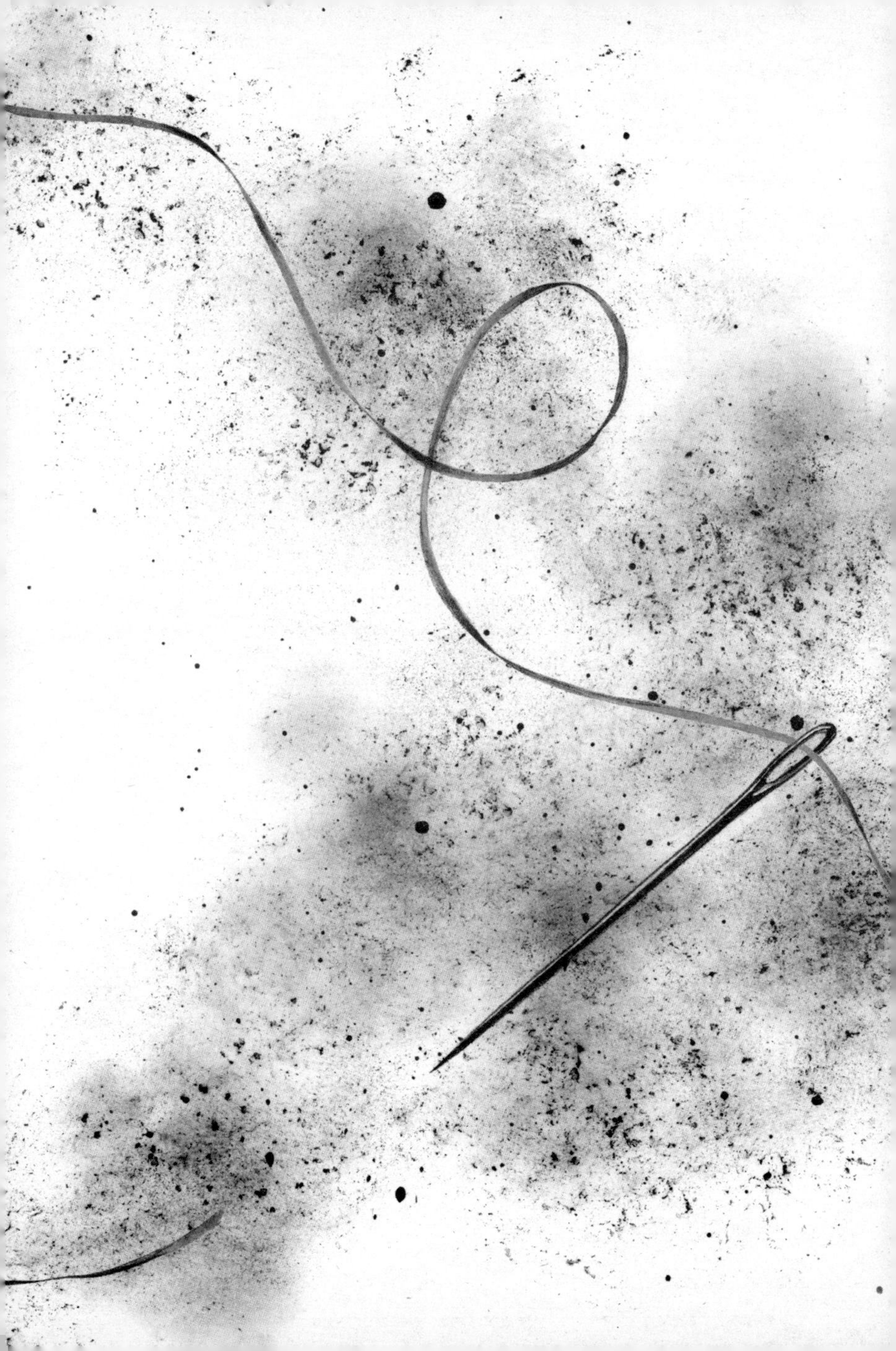

And then she was gone.

FORTY

SHE WATCHED THE child Thorn walking up the path to her front door.

Her mum was locking the car.

She'd had to come to school to pick her up after the fight at the swimming pool.

She watched the teenage Thorn walking up the path to her front door, schoolbag slouched over her shoulder.

Her mum was out at work.

She had her own key and her head was full of thoughts of dreamy, spotty Clive.

She watched the adult Thorn walking up the path to her front door, back home, after years.

She was knackered, defeated.

Her love had been taken away and she carried a bag with the clothes she would need, and the baby's clothes for when it arrived.

Then the sirens went.

The emergency alert screeched from everyone's mobile phones, ear-shattering, jarring, jolting, blaring, shocking.

People all over pulled the devices from their pockets, picked them up off their desks, rummaged through their clothes on the floor.

Air Raid. Seek Shelter. And it gave a list of locations at risk.

Child Thorn, teenage Thorn, adult Thorn, all ran for the house.

They didn't have a cellar. Hadn't dug shelters in the garden.

These things weren't necessary in a civilised country.

There was no tube station nearby. No communal concrete shelter built in the street.

They ran into the house.

Their mum was with them or she wasn't.

Their dad was home or he wasn't.

Gregor was there or he wasn't, was a kid or a youth or an adult, or he wasn't.

The drone of flying machines grew louder overhead, from the direction of elsewhere, and it came closer.

An explosion, thought Thorn as she watched all this. *That was how it began, that must be how it ends. But which one is this happening to?*

Was it all the dream of a child, witnessing a future that will never unfold?

Or do I live through this?

And then the sound cut out.

Silence in the sky.

And like a doodlebug the bomb fell, a fat black bird, dead and dropping, as she knew it would. Down, down, down at her house.

FORTY-ONE

AND THE WRECKAGE rose. And the dust plumed. And the thunder rolled. And the fire burned.

And the darkness engulfed. And the weight of everything crushed the life from the living.

FORTY-TWO

LATER.

Rescuers tried to dig.

There were too many houses and too few tired concrete shifters.

Night had fallen and rain had come.

It was slow going, and miserable with it.

The bricks and timbers, rubble and roof tiles, groaned and complained, moaned and wept, but the bodies hidden down, deep, darkly underneath stayed silent.

Maybe they found the cat first. Threw its broken body to one side.

It would land on a pile of sodden books, already shifted out the way, alongside the shattered bookcase.

Fire burned and rain poured, and perhaps Gregor, who had not been home, helped shift rubble, perhaps Clive came running.

ZERO, AGAIN

AND THORN.

And Thorn.

And Thorn.

She had found herself thrown backwards by the explosion, her hearing ringing, her vision pulsing and fuzzy. There was the taste of sewage and brick and petrol. Brick dust and fire. Night black and star bright. Cracks and splinters and the world saying nothing, nothing, nothing.

But she felt the tug of the red ribbon sewn through her side.

I'm dead, she thought. *Under all that, I'm dead.*

She shouldn't have to think this, to see this.

She knew it was the case.

She hoped it was the case.

To be trapped, in the dark, with knowledge as crushing as the building. That was too horrible a thought, too dreadful, too dark a thought. One she wouldn't wish on any living being, on any being of any sort. It was like drowning – her greatest fear, that suffocation of panic. No one pumping the air in. No one on the pumps. Helpless, helpless.

Poor Thorn.

But as the ringing faded and her vision returned, and as the smell of destruction lessened and lessened she came to find herself elsewhere, yet again.

Poor Thorn.

And she saw herself, saw her body lying in a hospital bed, except it wasn't her body. She'd made that mistake once before. This was her mum, younger, and with a hugely swollen belly.

And Thorn knew this was where it ended. And where it all began.

She had died. And she was about to be born.

A loop of self-consciousness.

A mind in the world.

A baby.

A way for the universe to sit up and make sense of itself, if only for a little bit, and if only in a small far-off corner of itself.

She had so much to look forward to, so many adventures, through dark and light. A life. With all the choices that entailed, the light and the dark. The choices. The people, the people, the people.

A life.

To live.

And with that thought, Thorn forgot everything and began again.

ABOUT THE AUTHOR

A.F. HARROLD is an English poet, performer and children's author. He has written the Fizzlebert Stump series, about a boy who lives in the circus and has suitably silly adventures, and the Greta Zargo duology, about a schoolgirl investigator who accidentally saves the world. Twice. His novel, *The Imaginary*, (illustrated by Emily Gravett) was made into a movie by Studio Ponoc and can be seen on Netflix. His novel, *The Song from Somewhere Else* (illustrated by Levi Pinfold), won the Amnesty International/CILIP Honour at the 2018 Carnegie awards.

He lives in Reading with a comedian, an author of historical fiction for kids, and a radio broadcaster (all the same person).

www.afharroldkids.com

ABOUT THE ILLUSTRATOR

MILLY CHAPPLE is an artist and illustrator from the Cotswolds. After studying Spanish and Portuguese at the University of Bristol, she combined her love of painting and storytelling and embarked on an MA in Children's Book Illustration at Cambridge School of Art.

When she's not illustrating, she enjoys reading, writing and adventuring to new places.

www.millychapple.com